ROY

Dennis Lightfoot

Cover Image:
freddie-marriage

Thanks to Mary G for publishing assistance.

Dedicated to those akin to Roy.

Have you ever wondered why certain events that occur along our life's path often dovetail into something quite unexpected? Is the journey we take simply random or might everything that happens be preordained? Are we watched over by some external influence that guides our destiny?

For some that are blessed with loving parents the journey through life can be sweet. But, for those born into a household without the fundamental basics of love and care the road to fulfilment may be loaded with stumbling blocks. What chance does any child have of finding happiness when their parents fail to nurture their offspring to the best of their ability?

Brian Ashworth was a blameless victim, born into a dysfunctional family, deprived of parental love in his formative years. By not receiving vital childhood affection in those early times, his life and learning would take many unexpected deviations. The path he travelled was one of 'learn as you go'. Then perhaps, one day, his fated destination may finally be reached.

Kenneth and Lucy

The often moody and hyper-volatile mother, Lucy, was unexpectedly pregnant. Developing in her womb, the innocence of her second son, Brian, a full fifteen years after the birth of her first.

Over the previous two years there had been a steady increase in her disturbed and somewhat neurotic behaviour that burdened an already shaky marriage to Kenneth. Lucy's constant petty arguments and the chilled air of derision undermined whatever love that remained.

As much as he tried Kenneth could no longer tolerate her uncontrollable mood swings. In an attempt to resolve the issue he recommended they both seek counselling. The mere suggestion caused more friction. Lucy vehemently refused to acknowledge that there were factors that needed to be addressed, then broke into another temper tantrum, accusing him of trying to manipulate her thoughts to suit his own agenda.

Rather than continue living in such disharmony with a total lack of loving affection and having already been banished into a separate bedroom for over five months, Brian's father reluctantly made a decision to abandon Lucy.

With only a suitcase crammed with clothing he vacated the home to seek a modicum of peace elsewhere. He hoped he might find direction without the stresses of being with a vexatious woman.

Ken took refuge with lodgings in a country town hotel. He

also deliberately isolated himself from friends and family to avoid accidently crossing her path.

After a fortnight of isolation the inner peace cleared his head. It became evident nothing could be gained by staying around any longer as there would be little benefit of him returning to the family.

His decision was to accept his fate and move interstate where better employment prospects were currently available. With a heavy heart Kenneth left the State and never returned to visit Lucy or to see the birth of his second son.

Brian's Journey

As the infant boy grew, his now sole-parent became increasingly embittered as each month passed.

"You are just like that rotten bastard of a father of yours," she would bellow at little Brian whenever anything went awry.

Young Brian's mere presence in the house now served as a constant reminder of her estranged husband. His much older brother had already scarpered from home a few months prior to Brian's birth when the disharmony between his parents became disturbingly evident.

A few weeks before the lads' fourth birthday, Lucy had met and sought solace with another man whose marriage that had also ended disastrously. A month later the new-found partner and his two daughters moved into her house. Young Brian was now a child surplus to requirements that no longer fitted into his mother's substituted life with her defacto and his girls. A decision was made for the young boy to be sent to his father. Unfortunately, his father's circumstances were such that he had scant time or the facilities to raise a young boy. When his mother vehemently refused to accept Brian back, the luckless lad was placed into a State-care institution.

With no contact from his mother and only sporadic visits by his father, Brian lived the life of an orphan. He remained in the children's home for the next five years until a caring uncle heard of his plight and had the primary-school-aged boy returned to his birthplace to be fostered by relatives.

Living firstly with his Aunt and Uncle, then with his older

brother and his wife, after that with his Grandparents, then back again to his brother.

Being shuttled around homes became an accepted way of life for the boy whose parents had disowned him. Apart from the inconvenience of constant relocation, life was not totally unpleasant. When the weather was unsuitable to go fishing with his uncle, Aunty taught him how to cook cakes and scones and make delicious soups. His brother taught him how to ride and maintain a motorbike, and how to shoot with a rifle and hunt rabbits. And Grandma's cream-filled sponge cakes were delicious.

Grandpa was old and frail but his mind was sharp and he possessed a unique insight gleaned from a life of adversity. Often Brian would sit on the back verandah and listen to his stories of the challenges that shaped Pa's life. Apart from the yarns of how he lived through the hard times of the Great Depression, and going to overseas to war, some of his tales would refer to another dimension of ones spirituality. The precise meaning of his narratives were too deep for the young lad to fully comprehend but the occasional snippet of his wisdom would find root in Brian's now teenage brian.

On one occasion Grandpa said to Brian, "Life can be a challenge without a mother and father. You must learn to love and be loved."

This single statement became firmly embedded in the deepest part of the lad's mind.

At the conclusion to almost every discussion Grandpa would finish with: "Remember this sonny - Never forget to listen to your guardian angel. That, young fellow, is the second most valuable piece of advice I can impart to you."

At fifteen Brian was on his own. The hard times of being an

unwanted child faded as the testosterone of youth pumped through his adolescent body. Forgotten were the times of being forced to live the previous years in the homes of relatives. Now he had full-time employment at a car component maker's factory and with a weekly pay packet and the independence of living in a rented flat. He was now ruler of his own destiny.

Those days of being disowned by his parents were erased by his new focus on girls and having fun. Top of his priority list was to start a relationship with one of the pretty girls that were among his circle of friends. But which one? None seem to attract his eye nor warrant a connection. For two years motor cycles and cars overrode the importance he had previously placed on the young ladies and their company he often yearned.

Being frugal and not having to spend any of his earned cash on a steady girlfriend Brian had over the months saved enough to purchase a second-hand motorbike. One of his workmates was selling his vintage Triumph Tiger 500 and had given Brian first option to buy the machine. An inspection was arranged to view the bike in his friend's family garage. While checking over the Triumph, out of curiosity, his mate's sister Suzanne, wandered in to observe what the boys were doing.

Was it love or lust at first sight for teenage Brian when he was introduced to Suzanne? Here was a girl that ticked every box on his ideal partner requirement list. To Brian, she was perfection in a package, in the form of a honey-blonde goddess, fashionably attired in the trend of the time, wearing a miniskirt that emphasized her tall, slender figure. Brian was immediately smitten by the young lady. Fortunately, Suzanne also had a mutual attraction for the well-muscled dark haired lad. Little wonder Brian regarded the stars to been in perfect alignment for him on that day and his guardian angel had guided her to him.

They began dating and enjoying the intimate adventures of a young couple in love. Blinded by his desire for her and a smidgen of manipulation by Suzanne, Brian lavished most of his meagre junior store-man's pay to please the young lady he worshipped. This was his naïve way of declaring his love to her. Suzanne soon became accustomed to his doting and expected the spending to continue. Using her feminine guile Suzanne persuaded Brian to foot the bill for a car, an engagement ring, followed a year or two later by a wedding, then a honeymoon that was paid by him.

After several years of marriage and employment at the vehicle component factory Brian realised that his modest wage plus the overtime, would never supply the income he needed to maintain Suzanne. With the extra expense of their two infant children, her reliance on Brian's generosity became increasingly demanding. In his own naïve way Brian clung on to his belief that giving her everything she asked was the way to show that he loved Suzanne and the girls.

To cover her wants, Brian sold his beloved motorbike and worked weekends on a second job, pumping fuel at the local service station. Two jobs meant even longer hours away from his wife and daughters. Their family life had become strained.

'Maybe if I found alternative and more highly paid employment I could still keep Suzanne satisfied' he considered. Next began his search for the ideal job. Every morning Brian made it his first task to read the employment vacancy section in the daily newspaper he had arranged to be delivered to their home. Many positions sounded close to his desired income level and choice of occupation, but none gave him the same feeling of mixing responsibility with adventure, as did the advertisement that was calling for more personnel to enlist in the Army.

From what he had read, he believed he could better provide for his family by joining the Armed Forces. With the generous taxation allowances the nett salary was much higher, so too were the risks. Suzanne was hesitant about the proposed change and vented her dismay when he initially suggested applying for Military service. That was until she sighted the pay schedule for men serving overseas. When it became clear that a regular sum of money would be deposited into their joint bank account her resistance faded. With the new found change of prospective the idea became actuality and Brian enlisted. After his boot-camp basic training was finished he completed more specialized courses in counter-terrorism. In the process was duly trained to the rank of Corporal before finally being sent overseas to serve in Afghanistan.

In Afghanistan, the occasional skirmish met on the unit's regular patrols across enemy territory initially had little effect on the Corporal's perspective. His logic was simple, he was a trained soldier and this was his job and such events were to be expected. That was until the day he and the other members of the platoon were on a mission to monitor Taliban activity in a remote village. Brian's world was to take a rapid nosedive into another dimension.

Unfortunately the platoon had been sighted by a well-armed enemy force. Over an hour he and the other men were pinned down under a barrage of rocket propelled grenades that blasted their position. One well aimed bomb exploded within a few metres of his surveillance post. A young Lance Corporal happened to be sheltering where the RPG landed and received an instant golden ticket to soldier's heaven. This was the Corporal Ashworth's first experience with a death of a comrade. Then in desperate bid to pull back to a safer position his platoon Sergeant was struck in the leg by a well-aimed projectile from a Taliban sniper rifle. Then in a terrifying struggle to retrieve his section leader Brian crawled across open ground. Bullets from the enemies automatic rifles splattered around him ricocheting off the rocks sending shrapnel fragments in all directions. When the pair were finally able to reach the protective cover of a low mud-brick wall Brian immediately began applying first aid to the Sergeants gaping wound to prevent further loss of blood in an attempt to save the NCO's life.

The adrenalin charged experiences of that day had totally altered his outlook on life. Those grisly images of witnessing a man dismembered by a grenade, dodging a hail of bullets, the frantic effort to save a mate, instantly created turmoil in his mind and a constant struggle to remain rational and in control of his reactions.

The medical evacuation of the platoon Sergeant had now opened a vacancy within the troop. Corporal Ashworth was next in line for a promotion to Sergeant. A higher rank would be an added bonus worth exploiting. His pay level would also to raise which meant more money for his wife and family. This was the purpose of enlisting. An advancement in rank also came with a proviso that his tour of duty in Afghanistan would be extended by six months. Rather than yield to the issues he was experiencing and exposed to be in need of therapy the newly promoted Sergeant contrived ways to disguise the conflict related anxieties from his superiors. He resorted to the pretence of being 'OK' by donning a brave face and mentally repeating to himself 'keep it together - keep it together'.

No matter how much bravado he displayed to those around him, he personally was in a state of denial. The stark reality of serving in that bloody war-zone had severely affected Brian's emotional state. Many nights he was plagued with a replay of that horrific day and of other confrontations against a well concealed enemy. A foe that would also lurk among local civilians. Never knowing who was or who the enemy wasn't, began to rattle Ashworth's nerves. When trying to sleep, any sound of a fast approaching motor vehicle or hearing Arabic voices would send shudders through his body causing him to jump up in panic. Then each morning he would repeat his mantra "keep it together – keep it together".

Having completed his prolonged tour of duty, Sergeant Brian Ashworth landed back in Australia physically unscathed but laden with the heavy millstone of deep psychological anxieties. Home to his wife and their two children, Louise who was now six and her four-year-old younger sister Maryanne.

Suzanne had waited many months for Brian's return to fulfil her pent-up desires. She was a young woman that yearned for a steamy Mills and Boone depiction of a heroic soldier ravaging her with erotic sex and romance, wild adventure and heaps of squanderable wealth. The image of 'her man' coming home as a fearless conqueror vanished within the first week of his arrival. She wanted more than he was able now to give.

Brian was fully aware he was not the attentive lover he was before departing to war. His sexual drive had significantly diminished – but not because Suzanne was unattractive or his love for her waned. He always saw her though rose tinted glasses and believed she still loved him and in time their nocturnal embraces would improve. It was the clutter in his mind that rendered him almost impotent.

He truly adored Suzanne and loved the girls and resorted to holding on to them the only way he could. To him the choice was clear. His priority was to conceal from his family all signs of post-traumatic stress, the same method he had done in Afghanistan using the 'keep it together mantra' to deceive those around him. Working long hours in his former store-man's job also aided in hiding his inner struggle. The added benefit was the overtime rates would help keep the money flowing. More than enough to meet the bills, house payments and her demands.

Extended hours at work once again meant less time for the family. Being absent for longer periods each day coupled with early starts and late finishes each day, offered him an excuse to dodge his marital duties. Suzanne failed to see the sacrifices Brian was making to support their family. Brian's conscience appeased itself by reasoning he was still a caring husband and father providing well for his household.

All too soon it had become obvious to Suzanne that Brian had problems and was avoiding her. She realised that he could not meet her carnal expectations. Now she was living with an ex-soldier that had psychological issues who was not able to fulfil any of her sensual hankerings. On more than one occasion a much frustrated Suzanne had berated him by saying that he was boring wimp and no longer a 'real' man.

Any attraction she previously had for him prior to his enlistment had vanished. Because he no longer could deliver what she expected, her desire for him as her partner rapidly faded. To her he was now inadequate and wanted him out of the marriage and out of her life.

Without warning, while Brian was at work, Suzanne packed her bags and with their two young children vacated their house and drove off in 'her' car to chase her dream life-style. The explanation was written in a short and simple note – "Brian, I am leaving so I can find myself, something I could not do while I was shackled to a dud like you."

This was the prelude to a dramatic change in Brian's circumstances. Although nothing could equal the violence of a war against a fanatical enemy whose sole objective was to destroy anyone that opposed their radicalised religious beliefs. This part of his life's journey would also be equally arduous, one of emotional experiences and overcoming tribulation. Soon he would have no home, no family and no possessions and little reason to continue living.

" 'Find Herself!!' – What in the hell did she mean by that," he kept asking himself for those first few days following her sudden departure. All of his efforts to contact her through her friends were met with the same answer – "Don't know – did you try the others?" It soon became apparent that he was being given the run-around from each one he approached. They had already been coerced by Suzanne not to divulge her whereabouts.

Then a few days later a new question arose. Brian received a visit from a local police officer who questioned him in regards to a complaint by Suzanne. One of domestic violence. Her claim was Brian had made several threats to harm her and she feared for safety.

"Why did she tell the authorities that I was threatening her and she had to stay in hiding?" The answer for that arrived in the form of a court order for him to have no contact with her and the children plus an added nasty of Suzanne being granted safe custody of the girls. It wasn't long before the bad luck trifecta also appeared.

On her pre-planned instructions, a furniture removal pantech-truck pulled into the driveway of the house. While Brian was away at his workplace, a couple of brawny workers and Suzanne totally cleared the entire house and garage of all contents.

Only items left behind were his clothes, an old army back-pack, a knife fork spoon and one of each plate. Stretching the outer limit of her generosity and compassionate heart Suzanne had also 'donated' a tea-towel, a roll of toilet paper and a cake of soap. That night the unfortunate Brian came home to a heart-breaking barren house.

His world crumbled as he tried to juggle work with sleepless nights spent on the lounge room carpet with the rucksack as a pillow.

It wasn't long before suicide was being contemplated.

'Why won't she contact me? How could she be so cruel? All we ever did was have a couple of minor disagreements over money'? 'Why did a magistrate hear only her side of the story'? These unanswered thoughts were playing with his head, keeping him awake with the other problems that were already bouncing around in his tortured mind.

Brian's work ethic had fallen short of his bosses expectations. He was warned to shape up within the week or ship out and find employment elsewhere.

The toll of constant sleepless nights wove itself into his further downfall. One Friday morning, not long after smoko, his supervisor found him asleep at his work station and reported it to the manager. That afternoon Brian was given the inglorious 'DCM' - "Don't come Monday".

As the weeks went by without a pay-packet, mortgage payments slid into arrears. Being jobless and alone sent him falling ever deeper into the dark chasm of depression. The burden became too much when he received a mortgagee demand for him to vacate the house. His estranged wife had manipulated a deal with the bank and taken over the loan account. Through his repayment defaulting, she had effectively removed Brian from any claim or right to be on the property.

All the money held in the two signature bank account had magically disappeared the day after Suzanne departed with a simple wave of her access card. Even the few friends they once shared, were poisoned against him by more of her mendacities.

Drenched with the feeling of being completely disempowered and totally alone, Brian made the decision that evening to end it all. 'An empty house, she can have it', he sarcastically jested to himself as he headed to the shed to get his old single shot rifle that he had hidden in the rafters. 'One shot is all I need', flashed through his mind as climb on top of the wooden work bench. His hand nervously fumbled in the darkness of the gable to locate the Lithgow. A shudder tingled down his spine as his fingers touched the cold steel of the barrel. In his grip was the weapon he used to hunt rabbits and shoot crows. Nervously he reminded himself that it took only a single headshot to kill his target.

"Just one shot in the head and it will be all over," he repeated to himself.

After climbing down off the bench Brian drew back the rifle's bolt and gave the chamber a habitual blow to remove any dust. "Now for the bullet," he muttered as the adrenalin started to raise in his body. In his tool box he had stashed a packet of cartridges. Looking around in the dimness he tried to locate the metal box. Like all of his other possessions that too was gone. "Bloody bitch", he screamed.

More adrenalin surged through his veins heightening his desire to finish the lethal deed.

"A rope, a rope I need a fucken rope," he yelled towards the shed roof as his agitation intensified. Like a man possessed his eyes searched the building for a rope. No rope or cord could be found. A wrenching pain tore at his innards, tears flooded his eyes as he walked aimlessly around the rear yard in search of something to use as a suicide noose. His legs crumbled under him when he realised there was nothing suitable to be used to take that final step.

The incoming darkness bore witness to the emotional wreck of a persecuted man that had done no wrong, sprawled on the back lawn sobbing in absolute grief. Eventually Brian staggered back inside the empty house where he collapsed into the foetal position on the lounge room floor and cried himself to sleep.

Throughout the night voices echoed in his mind, 'Hell hath no fury than that of a woman scorned' then another would reply, 'she was not scorned – out to get every bloody thing she can get.' 'Doesn't she have any feelings – how could she be so callous?' 'What had she told the girls?'

These notions tormented his head until the feeble light of dawn began to filter through the window. It was then his decision was made. He gathered his few clothes and crammed them into the backpack, walked out the front door into the chilly morning air. With one last look at the house he threw the bunch of door keys into a garden bush and walked away from what was once 'their' family home.

Not only was he now without a home he was also penniless with no possessions. Unable to afford a bond or rent-in-advance for a flat he approached the welfare system. The multitude of personal questions put forward by a seemingly insensitive interviewer frustrated the already emotionally tender Brian. Being of a proud disposition Brian had to muster the little inner strength he had left just to come with cap in hand to seek assistance. An overwhelming feeling of being insignificant and basically left to fend for himself shattered his self-worth when was told: "We just don't give out money to whoever comes through our door, you have to qualify for any assistance," stated by the arrogant pen-pusher. It was also inferred that due to having no fixed address, he would be ineligible to receive social benefits until he could provide one.

Devastated by the experience Brian rose from his seat opposite the obviously well-paid, comfortably living worker and walked out of the building whilst an indignant voice from behind him called, "But Sir, you have not completed the questionnaire."

Now the burden of life was overwhelming him. All Brian wanted now was to find a hole to crawl in and let the world go by while the deep lacerations of his broken heart might one-day heal.

A paranoia developed of people sniggering and whispering behind his back forced the hapless Brian into another decision. Leave this town, get away from the finger pointers and go to the city. Having no funds for a bus ticket he began hitch-hiking. With backpack in one hand and the other outstretched with the thumb skywards for over two hours he trudged the highway edge. Eventually he was fortunate to be asked if would like a lift, by a Good Samaritan that was also heading for the big-smoke.

A much relieved Brian thanked the driver as he buckled into the passenger seat. Rather than appear like a complete loser he then fibbed that his wallet had been stolen and was heading home totally cashless.

"Happy to have someone to talk to, these long trips get a bit boring," the driver replied. "Be glad to buy a lunch for you – rather I do that than have someone watch me eating – especially if they look hungry as you," he generously offered, sensing his passenger was having hard times.

Being homeless in the city was much harsher than anticipated by Brian. It was soon apparent a vagabond such as he, had to learn quickly or suffer. Parks, cemeteries, old buildings and anywhere that would provide some shelter at night became his world. His body weight plummeted his hair and beard grew and now he looked the part of down and out. Thankfully on some evenings there was nourishment available to prevent him from starvation, via the generosity of a few charity kitchens that provided the homeless with a basic meal.

On frosty nights, newspapers stuffed inside his shirt and trousers acted as insulation against the icy chill. Cardboard cartons became ground sheets in an effort to stop the cold and dampness that crept through to his bones. Unfortunately, there was no protection for him against bullies and callous louts that gained pleasure from punching and kicking his defenceless body while he slept. Some went as far as urinating over him then fleeing before he could retaliate in any form.

"Piss-pot, hobo, get a job and you filthy maggot," were terms these cowardly attackers often described him as being. He was none of these. He appeared grubby with the need of a shave and a good wash – but he was basically a heartbroken shell of a man now existing in his lonely world with the soul-destroying illness of depression – the dreaded Black Dog that had bitten many a returned soldier.

Late one night three drunken louts decided to give Brian more than the once-over. They found him sleeping in a dry creek bed that meandered its way through the parklands. After beating him to almost unconsciousness then pouring the dregs of their beer bottles over their weakened victim, decide it would be further fun to loosen the projecting earth ledge he had been forced under. One of the hero's pinned Brian to the ground with a broken tree branch while the others collapsed the sizeable mass of dirt onto his struggling body.

Had it not been for a leafy part of the branch that held him by the neck, his head would have also been covered under a ton and a half of soil. Having got their thrill of the despicable actions the oh-so-tough morons drunkenly staggered away laughing about their dastardly deed, leaving their victim trapped. Fortunately another homeless bloke that was hiding in some bushes nearby saw what had happened. He came to Brian's aid and frantically dug him out using only his bare hands? That Good Samaritan was another homeless soul named Jeff.

Jeff was also an ex-serviceman with post-traumatic stress disorder who had been living rough. From their short conversations Brian was able to glean that Jeff served as part of a special force team secretly attached to an American unit that entered Iraq and Kuwait to counteract the sands of discontent in the first Gulf War. Jeff refrained from elaborating on his experiences or the horrors he had also observed whilst with the Yanks. From his body language and minimal eye contact Brian gleaned that the bloke must have witnessed many atrocious that left him to grapple with a legacy of low self-esteem and a head full of torment too painful to discuss.

To maintain his low profile, Brian rarely spoke to anyone. The fear of being incarcerated he chose not to report the bullying episode to the police. Jeff was a few years older than Brian and had also fallen out of mainstream society and become non-communicative with the authorities. He resorted to alcohol to bury his personal emotional pains and had survived in a semi stupor each day with the aid of a bottle or cask of cheap Port wine and the occasional free feed at a soup kitchen.

A bond formed with between the two men. Despite not talking to others, the pair would greet each other warmly and occasionally enter into a brief conversation whenever their paths happened to cross. Unfortunately the usually not quite sober, alcohol breathed Jeff retold the same stories on most meeting. Over time, Brian pieced together from listening to Jeff's ravings that his father was a wealthy business man who owned a chain of book stores. He dis-owned his son when Jeff refused to give up the grog and work with him in the business. Even though Jeff's stories about his father were repetitive Brian shared the common bond of being homeless and felt he owed a debt of gratitude for rescuing him.

For several weeks Brian had roamed the alleys and streets without encountering Jeff. Trying to take a shortcut back to the parklands where he assumed Jeff would be, he had wandered into what obviously was the wealthier part of the city. The properties here were mainly imposing two storey houses sited behind well-maintained gardens, manicured lawns and wide paved driveways leading to impressive garages with expensive luxury motor vehicles parked in front. It was evident to Brian this area was exclusively for the elite professionals with fattened bank accounts.

For a bum like himself the area was a definite 'no-go zone' for down and outs. This part of town would certainly be where the police would patrol on a regular basis and send any homeless folk packing with strict orders to never to return. Suppose it might be called a "shielding the rich from reality" exercise sanctioned by the police hierarchy for their well-to-do Champagne and Vintage Port drinking affluent chums.

With the dreaded thought of being in the wrong place he turned to retrace his steps to withdraw from the area he had subconsciously nick-named Poshville. Brian had only taken a few steps in retreat when he heard a vehicle approaching along the tree lined avenue where he had inadvertently meandered. Without looking to confirm if it were the police and not wanting to be confronted by the law Brian squeezed himself into a small hollow of the tall Cypress Pine hedge adjacent to where he was standing. In order to remain unseen he pressed his body deep among the branches and remained motionless until the vehicle passed.

Being wedged so far into the hedge he could now view the rear yard of the house and yard that the hedge shrouded from the street. By holding back one of the branches was able to spot a quaint wooden cabin tucked in behind a densely planted row of Candle Pines guarding the humble structure. These tall slender trees reminded Brian of a platoon of soldiers standing rigidly at attention while on parade. By moving further inward through the hedge he could see old cob-webs draping across the doorway to the hut. Dust coated window panes stood testament that it was probably disused and not having been visited for quite some time.

With eyes and ears alert much the same as if he was practicing an army manoeuvre he silently eased himself completely through the outer branches into the yard. Naively his logic was that here is a place he could not be sighted from any direction. The pines, the hedge and a high fence behind the cabin hid him and his discovery. Fully aware he was now a trespasser, the thought that this place could be a secret haven he might use as a squat, flashed across his mind.

Suddenly he froze in fear with an expectation that a person or property owners dog may at any moment come charging through the trees. His ears scanned for the slightest hint of a sound. Nothing. Just the faint whisper of the breeze through the foliage. A feeling of being safe, at least for the moment permeated his body, one similar to the relief felt after having cleared an area of enemies back in Afghanistan.

Lowering his body and creeping cautiously as if on an army training manoeuvre, he edged closer to the cabin. As he neared the verandah he noted the door had provision for a padlock. There wasn't one. Silently he slipped the padbolt back. With the expectation the hinges would squeak, gently pushed the door slightly ajar. Only the sound of snapping overstretched spider-webs was heard as he continued to open the door wide enough so he could ease his body inside.

This was no ordinary garden shed – housing neither flower pots, nor wheel barrow or any other useful garden tools. The wooden floored interior was dustless and dry. Under the window stood a multi-drawer desk with a swivel chair parked in the leg space section. To his right at one end of the cabin door a fabric covered sofa with a single matching cloth cushion occupied almost the entire width of the structure. On the left, attached to the wall was a wooden shelf holding a dozen or so books haphazardly propped against each other. Closer inspection revealed many were dictionaries in various languages, a thesaurus and a few poetry books. Must have been a writer's retreat he mused as he sat his butt on the sofa and pulled the lonely cushion toward himself.

Brian was well aware that he was trespassing yet disregarded his conscience alerting him to the fact. Living rough had denied him any small luxuries such as a sofa and the risk involved for a few minutes of comfort he construed as being a deserved reward. It had been over a year and a half since he had sat on something so comfortable and with the feel of such security. Placing a cushion for his head, he lay down and began to wonder if this little cabin was once where a famous author penned his stories. With the quietness, the comfort of the sofa and that wonderful sense of security he soon fell asleep.

Hour after hour he slept. The longest uninterrupted and deepest sleep he had managed in many months. In his reveries he was back home with the wife and family living happily together. Days on the beach and riding new bicycles with the daughters were relived in his fantasy dream. In another realistic dream he was an accepted pillar of society – a writer, surrounded by books in a splendid house with a retreat cabin in the rear of the large garden.

Startled by the drone of engine noise close-by, he jolted upright in panic. His mind raced with flashbacks of being at war. Any sound similar to approaching enemy armoured vehicles and the fear of an impending attack, he hurriedly bolted out of the hut and hid among the shrubbery. From his position he realised he was still in the hut garden. From the bushes he could observe almost the entirety of a large lawned area that was at the rear of the owner's house. The source of the motor sound was the gardener that was driving his ride-on mower around in ever decreasing circles as he manicured the grass. It was obvious this was not the property resident but a lawn mowing contractor. Bob's Mowing Service logo on the driver's shirt and the painted sign on the mower, reassured him of that. Within minutes the mower-man and his noisy machine were gone and peace returned to the garden.

Pangs of hunger wrenched at his stomach. Brian had slept so soundly he missed receiving a morning feed at the hand-out charity. It was now over 30 hours since he had partaken of food. Sometimes the angels smile upon people – even the down and out.

Brian was looking for an easier way through the hedge trees to get back onto the avenue he had walked the previous day. It was then he spied what he recognised as a pear tree. This necessitated an immediate search among its branches in hope of finding a piece of fruit. Alas there were none.

Whilst scanning the pear tree he happened to notice a gap in the hedge through which he could climb to return outside the property. However it was a tight space and he would need to squat down low to squeeze through. With his body in the crouch position and about to push forward he almost squashed a ripe windfall pear that lay on the ground. Dusting off the dirt, then giving the pear a rub on the slightly cleaner inside lining of his coat the piece of fruit was ready to eat. How delicious it tasted. Sweet and juicy – the nicest pear he had ever eaten? Or maybe it was just his hunger that emphasized the flavour!

When he was once more again outside the property a weird sensation flooded through his body as he hastened to depart from the 'posh' neighbourhood. It was evident something had also changed in his thoughts. Was it the dream of books or was it the earlier images of sharing time with his children? Whatever it was, he now had a peculiar sense of feeling different. No longer the victim but a person again. A realization that it was time for his life to change had emanated within that hut. The big question for Brian - was how and why?

'Get clean, must get clean' the internal dialogue in his head echoed repeatedly. From experience he knew the location of every public convenience in the area and made a bee-line for the closest and cleanest one. Fortunately for him there was liquid soap and paper towel provided that he could use. Five minutes of lather and rinsing his face neck and armpits had him feeling refreshed and clean. His once unkempt unshaven facial hair had grown into a passable beard that needed just few quick strokes of the hand to have it looking respectable. Problem was now he could now smell the odour of his grimy coat. That had to go. The shabby rag was rolled up tightly and jammed into a plastic shopping bag he always carried in his back pocket, then stashed under a clump of bushes where he knew it could be retrieve if ever needed again when the cold weather returned.

A single pear was scant nourishment for one not haven't eaten for over a full day. By mid afternoon the gnawing gremlins were viciously attacking his stomach. Being in close vicinity of the local charity food kitchen Brian considered it may be worth an attempt to possibly have an early meal.

As he approached the gateway he was met by one of the volunteer staff. Was this a chance meeting or part of a guardian angels plot to 'save' him?

"You are a tad early – meals are not served until six," the

woman blurted at him.

Instead of telling the truth about being hungry he stammered (a nervous condition he developed in the Army when his mind held negative thoughts about his safety or well-being). – "I-I- I thought I might be able to lend a hand by doing dishes or something."

"As a matter of fact we do need some help," she replied - "One lady is unable to assist today and we could certainly do with and extra pair of hands – you will have to wear an apron over your clothes – hygiene precautions you know."

Luck happened that it was the kitchen workers afternoon tea time when he and the woman entered the building.

"Look at them feeding their faces," she said to her nervous recruit while passing him a clean apron. "By the way I'm Margaret, one of the supervisors of this place – everyone calls me Maggie and behind my back they refer to me as Major."

"What should we call you?" came next as she slipped the halter of her apron over her head.

"B-Brian," he nervously replied.

Then in a Sergeant-like voice Marg announce to the other workers, "Attention everyone, Laura cannot come in today, she is having the day off so she can take her mother to hospital for some minor surgery. However we are fortunate enough to have a replacement, this is Brian, and he will be washing pots and pans for us." Then Marg said in a more subdued tone to Brian, as she pushed a plate of freshly made sandwiches towards him, "Grab yourself a sandwich or two and have a cuppa – can't have you working on an empty stomach."

It did not take long for Brian to remember the old phrase, 'There is no such thing as a free lunch'.

For him this was a new experience of being on the staff side of the charity, instead of standing in line among the other unfortunates waiting to be served a free meal without having to work for one. No wonder they were grateful to have someone to wash dishes. As fast as he had cleaned one stack, another pile would be dumped on the washbowl counter. After the plates came a seemingly never ending stream of pots, pans and trays. This was continuous for the next two hours. Not until then was he able to take a well-earned break.

"Looks like they threw you into the deep end. We had a lot more mouths to feed today. Caught us all by surprise. Better take a rest and sit down and have the food we put aside for you," one of the elderly ladies said as she ushered him to a seat, placed the meal down on the table then left him to eat.

As Brian wiped the last smear of mashed potato and gravy from his plate the woman returned. In a polite English accent she enquired, "Where are you from?" while continuing to clean the adjacent table tops with a cloth, then added, "I thought I may have seen you in the meals line-up. You look more like a country boy than the other city ones. Perhaps I should introduce myself – I'm Louise Williams, but everyone just calls me Lou," she said with one finger tapping the name badge positioned on the shoulder strap of her apron.

Brian's eyes shifted toward her name tag then paused for a moment before he answered. "You guessed correctly – I am from the country."

"I can always tell – country men always stand much prouder than those from the city," Lou replied then looked into his eyes and asked, "Do you have a place to stay?"

Not wanting to reveal that he had recently found the hut he answered, "Yes – I have a place not far from here."

"Should you ever need to find another place let me know – I

am sure we can find somewhere nice for you," Louise said while taking his plate from the table.

Fate often weaves a web of mysterious events to achieve an outcome. The charity kitchen was about to close, his hunger was well sated and nights darkness was already into its first hour, he headed towards the cabin to sleep the night. As he neared the avenue corner a slow moving patrolling police car pulled alongside him.

"Do you live around here?" the copper in the passenger seat politely enquired through his open window.

All hell broke out in Brian's mind. 'What do I say, what should I say?' then without thinking things through, he stammered a nervous, "J-Just finished doing my bit for society - working at the Charity Kitchen and now heading home – I'm staying with my Aunt, d-down the road a bit."

The policeman looked at him then said, "Got quite a few homeless bums squatting near here, s'pose you saw many of them tonight looking for a free feed – might pay you to get rid of the beard you almost look like one yourself!"

Luckily (or was it?) the patrol car then received an urgent radio message and set off in pursuit of whatever felon they had to chase. Brian stood there stroking his beard and gave a polite wave to the officers as they did. "Shit!! That was close," he muttered to himself.

Getting through the hedge was harder at night than he anticipated. Shadows disguised the openings, it took some time to find the gap he had previously utilised. Eventually the same tight spot that access was gained on the first occasion was found. As he emerged on the other side he noticed the faint glow of a light shining from an upstairs window of the house which he then saw switch off. The dreaded thought that somebody does live here flashed through his mind and he almost retreated to the street. But the lure of a soft bed urged him forward again.

Brian looked around nervously as he was about to carefully lift the padbolt. Thankfully once again it made no sound nor did the old door hinges.

An overwhelming sense of security dispatched all other thoughts as he settled on the sofa. A day full of a variety of stresses that started with being jolted awake, getting clean, scrubbing pots and pans, dishwashing and the brush with the police sent him into a deep sleep within moments of placing the cushion under his head.

Next morning Brian awoke to the raucous chatter of several Magpies presumably arguing over territory. Instead of beating a hasty departure from the hut he surveyed the garden through the small window. After noting that the area was devoid of any impending intrusion he selected a book of verse from the shelf then eased himself into the swivel chair.

Thumbing through the pages he noticed that this was a collection of poems by a writer with the initials GRW. Occasionally he paused and read the first line or two of a verse. A peculiar sensation of feeling that the words were speaking directly to him caused him to slam the book shut. Spooky!! He thought, then reopened the pages then read a few more lines. 'Along life's path we travel never knowing what each day will set before us' then, 'many a mile of uncertainty along a winding road', then a few lines down 'adversity leads to compassion, compassion evolves into caring, caring yields to love' and another line that challenged his thoughts, 'to discover oneself precedes happiness'.

Brian sat and pondered the snippets of verse dwelling on the two words 'discover oneself'. "How do I do that?" he repetitively quizzed himself. His mind momentarily flashed back to the ex's words of wanting to 'find' herself. A sudden rumbling in his belly brought him to the realisation that food would be more important than philosophy at this moment in time. After a quick face wash and a swig of water courtesy of a garden tap he found located behind the hut, he squeezed himself through the hedge and was back out on the avenue.

With no particular destination in mind, Brian wondered if he would still be required to wash dishes at the charity, so headed in that direction.

On arrival the place seemed deserted. His knocking on the main door was met with empty echoes from the large hallway. When he raised his hand to give a final knock, Louise came trundling up the path heading towards him.

"Knock as much as you want – no one is there ye,t" she chuckled as she inserted a key into the lock. "It's Maggie's day off and my turn to open today – the others will be along later." She tugged at Brian's arm for him to enter the building. "Better pop the kettle on and we'll begin with a nice cuppa and perhaps a slice of toast or two before we start – you have come to help I hope?" she added.

It was not Brian's intention of working - he still had the 'discover oneself' notions rattling in his head. Rather than say no, he went with the flow and agreed to assist with the meal preparation for that day. His grumbling stomach was sated after devouring 4 slices of thickly spread Vegemite on hot toast washed down with two cups of tea. Louise was somewhat sergeant-like in the way she controlled some of the later arriving volunteer staff with her do-this do-that commands.

These were never directed at Brian. Whenever Lou barked an order she would turn and wink at Brian as if to say, 'they' were working as a team.

After a full day of preparing meals, cleaning plates and utensils Brian realised how hard the unpaid helpers did work. Except for his meal breaks the work was consistent, only ceasing after the last homeless soul had been fed and vacated the premises. Once back 'home' in the hut he reflected how tough he thought being homeless appeared. Being a helper was just as arduous except in a very different way. Being supplied three meals in one day sent twinges of guilt into his musing as he pondered on the single feed he occasionally received only a week ago.

The importance of looking respectable was now a priority. After neatly folding his trousers to prevent any further creasing he settled down on 'his' bed - the sofa. Ideas of how to bridge the gap between the down-trodden and a new found respect for those with enough time on their hands to make themselves available for community service held his thoughts as he drifted into a deep sleep.

Again the similar dream of being a famous writer and shelves of books filled the moments before he awakened. As he opened his eyes his immediate thought was "I have never written anything that made sense – so how could I become a renowned author – why do I dream that constant dream – what do all the books represent or mean"?

For the first time in ages, life seemed to be moving in a positive direction for Brian. Social Services had finally decided that he was now eligible for minimal support by their recognition of his volunteer work. Soon payments would be made to his old personal bank account. Fortunately for him it was kept open thanks to the grand total of three dollars and twenty-six cents that was inadvertently left held in the balance. Providence had supplied him three meals a day, a soft warm sofa, a modest stipend and some fresh clothes thanks to Lou recognizing that he was of similar build to her deceased husband, Roy.

"Got two robes full of his stuff and would like to see it gone," she announced, as the parcel was handed to him earlier at the charity centre.

On Wednesday Brian came to work wearing Lou's husband's trousers and shirt.

"Nice fit – I reckoned my Roy and you were about the same size. Good to see them being used again," Lou said when she spotted Brian in his new garb. "I still have heaps of his stuff in the house and also have Roy's BMW motorbike in the shed. It has been there for the past seven years. Never got round to selling it – had lots of sentimental value in for me. Roy and I would go for a ride every Sunday afternoon. Can you ride a big motorbike?" she asked, then sighed as she remembered those outings.

His motorbike license had not yet expired. It was one of the few items he had kept with him since the day he walked away from the house. Brian was a tad unsure as to whether he should let on that he held a valid license, just in case Lou wanted him to take her for a ride one Sunday. He paused for a moment then answered her question.

"As a matter of fact – I did once have a motorbike and rode to work before I joined the Army. Then the bike wasn't much use to me so I sold it. Wish I never had. Still have a current license and yes I can ride."

"Perhaps you can come and start my Roy's bike for me.

Regularly I would start it up most Sunday afternoons – just like we did when he was alive. I simply turned the key and pressed the starter button to get it going then let the motor warm up before I switched it off. It won't turn over now. I think the battery is flat or needs replacing, not sure which. My legs are not as strong as his so I couldn't kick start it like he did. I would appreciate you coming by and checking it out for me," Lou said, and she once again released a sigh, reminiscing about her late husband dressed in his leathers and helmet.

Brian hesitated at giving an answer. Lou was in her late sixties and this gave him some cause for concern. Sixty something and sitting pillion seat on a motorbike. In his mind he had visions of Lou in leathers with her grey hair and wrinkled face being blown by the wind as the bike sped along the highway.

Brian was about to make an excuse as to why he possibly could not, when Lou interrupted his thoughts and said. "I'm afraid I can't go for any more rides – might need a hip replacement in the near future – couldn't possibly get on the machine nowadays."

This threw a completely new light on the subject. "Sorry to hear that Lou, and yes I would be glad to take a look at what is wrong with the battery. Let me know when and where you live and I will make some time to check it out."

"Thank you, Brian – Roy will be so pleased if it gets started again. This weekend would be a good time – can you make it on Sunday? Whoops nearly forgot – I live just off the Avenue the double storey house with the big Cypress hedge on the Avenue side - number two Alexander Street."

Brian stood stunned for a moment – this was the house in front of the garden shed in which he had been sleeping. The thought of, "I wonder if she knows?" rocketed through his mind. If she did, nothing was ever said or indicated by Lou, he reflected as he decided whether to help or not.

Nervously Brian replied. "S- S-Sunday" he stuttered. "W-What time?" he added in a slightly more composed manner.

"Any time after lunch would be best for me – I go to church in the mornings," Lou replied, then added, "Will you be able to find the place? - it's not far from here".

Hearing her say that eased the tension in his thinking. Maybe she doesn't know! "One o'clock – Yeh, one o'clock I'll be there if that is OK with you."

"See you at one then," Lou cheerily responded as she walked towards door.

Rather than raise any suspicions as to where he was living, Brian left the garden shed earlier than usual the next Sunday morning. By doing this he thought the probability of accidently 'meeting' with Lou would be greatly lessened. With nearly six hours to go before his appointment with the BMW, he decided a walk to the riverbank was the best option for 'wasting' away time.

It was now early autumn. The sun still had a bit of sting in its rays. On the riverbank were several large shady trees with park benches underneath on which a visitor could rest. Brian opted to sit and relax on the seat overlooking an open lawned area. The early start combined with the warm fresh air and the quietness of the place made Brian drowsy and soon drifted asleep. A spooky feeling woke him. He imagined he was dreaming and could hear two very familiar voices – those of his estranged daughters. Suddenly he realised this was no dream, he could hear and see them not far from where he sat. An immediate impulse to jump up and go to them was stifled. The shock of them being so near had him glued to his seat. Then he noticed his ex, sitting on the lawn holding a young baby in her arms with man he did not recognise alongside her.

Emotions of fear, anger, and jealousy swept over him. The joy of sighting his girls was blown to pieces by the presence of the baby and the 'other' man. For several minutes his heart thumped rapidly beneath his shirt while dozens of options raced through his thoughts. "W, W, What should I do?" he asked himself.

Before he could decide whether it would be wise to move any closer, all those he were watching began to walk away. 'She' was carrying the baby while the girls walked each side of the man holding his hands. His daughters seemingly happy to be holding the hand of someone else.

The 'family' piled into a car parked nearby then drove away. In less than a moment they had gone. Brian felt sick, his stomach became agitated, almost to the point of him vomiting. His world once again fell into a hole. They were so close and he was not noticed at all. It was as if he had become invisible or worse – totally forgotten.

That single brief episode had destroyed the many good factors that were returning into his shattered life. The box of despair had been reopened and dreaded Black Dog was again growling at his heels. Over and over his mind regurgitated past events of the separation from both wife and children. This uninvited episode ignited similar feeling to those of being under attack in Afghanistan. Panic began churning in his now chaotic mind. Once again he was trapped by an unseen enemy whose sole intent was to destroy him. Needless to say, all ideas of taking a look at Lou's motorcycle were for now thrust away.

For the remainder of the afternoon Brian wandered

aimlessly. Neither stopping to eat or drink. Once again his mind was constantly plagued by those inner voices he desperately fought to escape. Evening found him back sitting on the river-edge park bench in vain hope the children might return. The incoming chill of nightfall and the lack of food or water shook him into the real world, realizing the need for a warm bed. As he moseyed 'home' his mind was also full of remorse for failing to have met the appointment with Lou and for not showing up for food serving at the charity. In that one day life went from being pleasant, to absolute disaster. He was once again laden with the depressive thoughts he had suppressed for so long. Emotions of guilt and vulnerability had returned and clouded his thinking.

Being unable to sleep longer than a few minutes at a time, coupled with weird dreams, added to Brian's struggle to regain his mental composure. It was not until the first light of dawn began to creep into the cabin he was finally able to fall into a much needed sleep.

That Sunday had sapped every ounce of joy from his spirit. Lack of food could be rectified with a meal. Seeing and being unable to communicate with his girls, catapulted him into that deep black hole of feeling worthless. Monday came and went. All that Brian had to eat for the day was a few crumbly biscuits left over from the charity worker's afternoon tea, held earlier that week. Food was not an immediate priority. The prolonged hours of existing solely within the realm of a tortured mind had depleted his gusto. A pressing need for more sleep overrode any nourishment desire.

As his bleary eyes opened on the morning of the following day, pangs of hunger and thirst chewed at his gut. Sustenance was now a priority. With a heavy heart and a bundle of negative thoughts, he dressed then went outside and splashed his face with hands full of cold water of the garden tap. The shock of chilled water snapped him into a modicum of awareness. The time had arrived to decide if he would be brave enough to face those at the goodwill centre, especially Lou.

"You do not look well," Maggie said as a sheepish Brian took his work apron from the hook. Then she added, "Lou said you never came to check the motorbike on Sunday nor turned up to help yesterday and was worried why – we don't seem to have an address or number for contacting you."

Rather than be put on the spot and giving away his details Brian quickly change the subject and raised the question, "Will Lou be in today?"

"No, Lou will not be here to help – her son is coming to visit her and they are going out for dinner – she will be here tomorrow," replied Maggie. Before she was able to say anything more, Brian threw in a diversionary question. "Would you like a cup of tea or coffee Mag – I could do with a nice strong coffee right now," then when her back was turned, pounced on a plate of biscuits to appease the imaginary worms that were gnawing at his empty intestines.

Interaction with others plus a nourishing feed had partially eliminated the residual hub-bub that had bounced uncontrollably around in his brian the previous few days. His mindset had become more settled by the time he headed for 'home'. As he walked there was the occasional moment when his thoughts slithered into a replay of seeing his daughters. These repeats almost set the cogs of his mind churning again. "Think of something else – think of something else" he repeated to prevent himself from falling into the abyss of mental torture he had endured over the preceding days.

Arriving 'home', and having settled in the hut, that strange unexplainable sensation of peace cleared his thinking. Brian's thoughts then changed from negativity to compassion. A mild guilt feeling permeated his thoughts. 'I should be hoping that the girls and their mother are happy. It is selfish of me to desire to possess them. It would be wrong not to want for their lives to be more fulfilling. Perhaps I was not such a great Dad after all,' he said to himself, as he lay on the sofa cogitating the limited times he shared with his daughters. In less than two minutes his physically and emotionally tired body slipped into another much needed slumber.

A loud throaty exhaust roar of a motorbike being revved somewhere close abruptly woke Brian next morning. The sun was shining bright, his eyes took a few moments to focus. Again and again the bikes engine was revved up then bought back to idle. This enabled Brian to locate the source of the sound – It was coming from Lou's garage. 'Seems the son has stayed overnight and has got the Beamer going - she won't be needing me to start it for her', Brian muttered as he hurriedly tidied himself enough to be presentable at work. As his hand was about to clasp the door handle a thought bubble popped into his thinking. 'It would be a bloody good idea to bag up and stash his meagre worldly possessions under a nearby tree just in case the son was curious enough to look into the cabin'. Grabbing whatever was in view then shoving the pieces into two shopping bags he vacated the hut.

At the charity Brian was busy stacking dishes when a cheery Lou arrived. "How are you today – thought you may have been unwell? I reckoned it would take some sort of sickness to stop you from turning up for a day's hard labour." She said in a jolly tone then added, "As luck happens my son knows a bit about motors and he was able to get the motorbike going again – thanks for your offer." She then busied herself preparing the tables for the day's meals.

"I was a bit off colour for the past few days and felt guilty for not letting you know I was not coming to help as I usually do," Brian said as Lou brushed passed him carrying some soiled tablecloths. "Glad to hear the bike is going again." This was no fib he chuckled to himself as he had actually heard the motor being revved.

Then as Lou walked passed in the opposite direction carrying an arm full of fresh table covers she said, "Any time you would like to have a ride on it let me know – my son said the carburettor probably needs a cleanout and a long drive would do it a heap of good." She busied herself again with the tables.

"Will do and thanks," was Brian's reply.

Several days of going to work and presuming that Lou had not caught on that he was camping in her hut had Brian feeling optimistic again. Might as well take Lou up on her offer to take the BMW for a ride he contemplated and when the opportunity arose to ask Lou, Brian put in his request.

"You certainly can Brian" was her response "I am sure Roy's leathers and helmet will fit you – it will be like seeing him again with his other love – his motorbike. With a bit of luck his boots might fit you as well, and that would make the job complete." Lou added as she looked down at Brian's feet. "Would you like to take it for a run this Sunday when I go to Church? Maybe you can give me lift there – wouldn't that have the congregation gossiping – only joking," she said with a grin, to which Brian replied:

"OK, Sunday morning it is."

No one could have asked for a better day that Sunday, the sun was warm, no wind, and the roads were dry, perfect weather for a ride. Lou purposely busied herself in the garden while Brian dressed in the garage in Roy's leathers and boots. He then wheeled the machine outside and was just about to put on the helmet when Lou said "Smile" and sneaked in a photo shot of Brian standing alongside the BMW.

"I'll get this one printed off to compare you with my Roy," she giggled as she looked down to review the picture on her digital camera.

"You're lucky the camera didn't break – I'm not photogenic at all," Brian replied as he positioned himself astride the bike then hit the starter button. The motor immediately responded and fired up. Then, with a few tweaks of the throttle by Brian - just to stimulate the exhaust to give out that growl only BMWs can make and to give Lou a bit of 'remember when', Brian flicked down the visor on the helmet and with a wave to Lou, set out on his ride showing off his handling skills with deliberate quick changes through the first three gears.

In the rear vision mirror Brian could see Lou waving to him as he turned the corner onto the Avenue. This is just what the doctor ordered, he mused as he tapped the bike into fourth then fifth gear. A pang of regret flashed across his thoughts as he recalled giving up his old machine to lessen any financial burden on his young family. Those memories quickly faded as the bike was turned onto the express way. Now he could give the bike the run it needed as the speed limit was 100 kph.

Brian was in his element – the rush of the wind flowing over his helmet and that throaty roar of the bike's exhaust. A quick check of the fuel gauge and with a hasty calculation realised that he could only travel a few more kilometres at this speed then eased back on the throttle and enjoyed the ride.

Back at Lou's, Brian excitedly thanked her for the opportunity of being able to give Roy's machine a run. Louise saw the genuine happiness in his smiling face and could see how much Brian had appreciated the chance to ride and his fondness of motorbikes. For a moment she stood and watched as Brian unzipped then removed her late husband's leather jacket and reflected on just how much this man resembled Roy and his love of two-wheel freedom. Then, as Brian was again thanking her for letting him take the BMW for a spin and about to hand the jacket back to Lou and she made a split-second decision and looked Brian in the eyes.

She said, "You can keep the jacket and other gear – they fit you so well – I am sure Roy would agree."

Lou then took the two steps towards the bike and removed the keys and held them out to Brian. "I want you to have the bike – then you have the complete package – leathers and a helmet are of no use unless you have something to ride and I could see the delight in your eyes after you returned from your little outing."

Brian stood with his mouth agape, unable to think what to say. Then went into an apologetic mode and humbly replied, "I can't pay you for it – I don't have any money, I couldn't raise anywhere near what it is worth," he said, while slowly shaking his head from side to side.

Lou looked him in the eye and countered his apologetic reasons. "You won't have to pay a penny, it is a gift. I am quite sure my Roy would agree to that too – it was destined for you to have. Now every time I see you with it, I will think of Roy. The two of you are so similar. You really do look like him in his younger days, especially when you are all kitted up and sitting on the machine. That is why I – or should I say 'we' - want you to have the bike. I have no doubt that Roy would only want his precious BMW to go to someone who will look after it and get pleasure from it as much as he did."

Louise's generosity posed a problem for Brian. How could he explain that he was 'camping' in the hut at the rear of her home? Should he tell her or keep hiding the truth about his homelessness? With these guilt's rushing through his mind Brian stood staring at the bike until Lou intervened.

"You don't seem too happy about having it."

"S-S-Sorry," Brian nervously stammered. "I was just thinking about where I could keep the bike as I don't have anywhere safe to park it."

"Why not keep it here in the garage – I'll give you a key to the door so that you can take it out whenever you want," then she paused before she dropped a bombshell; "I know you're squatting in my hut – I knew from the very first day. I saw you from my upstairs window."

Brian's face turned as red as a stop-light. "Y-Y-You never said anything," Brian sheepishly replied.

"To tell you the truth," Lou began, "At first I thought you were Roy – from a distance you looked the spitting image of him – to let you stay gave me comfort having 'him' around. I could never have asked you to leave. It would have been too painful to put someone out on the street who reminded me so much of him. I feel that the spirit of Roy lives in that little cabin – he loved its peacefulness and always said there is a 'strange contentment' that you feel when inside it."

Tears welled up in Lou's eyes.

Instinctive Brian wrapped his arms around her and gave a lingering hug. He could feel her pain of how she missed her husband.

"You must have loved him so much," Brian said softly as he released his arms and then held her hand. For a time they stood looking at the bike, both immersed in their personal thought of losing a loved one.

Lou broke the silence. "Brian please stay, just knowing you are nearby is reassuring for me. The feeling of security I get is worth far more than not having you here. You can even use the bathroom that we had built on the back of this garage. It was made for our son who lived here in his caravan for a few months. The van was parked alongside and close enough to its door so that he did not have to go into the house to use the loo, quite handy when it was rainy."

At Lou's request Brian stayed in the hut. Now he could walk down the house driveway instead of creeping through a gap in the hedge. There were no more trips to a public lavatory to clean-up. With this freedom he felt there was now more reason to live. Those melancholy teary moments of sadness that often haunted him, for the while abated. The now regular weekend rides on the BMW also added to his self-confidence and overall outlook.

Rather than trying to be a part of Brian's daily life Lou gave him the freedom to retain his independence - except for the occasions when she left some sheets or blankets and the odd piece of her Roy's clothing at his door.

Brian continued doing his volunteer work for the needy. Apart from personal satisfaction of doing something worthwhile, his only reward from the charity was the meals he received. Life now had meaning. It seemed that beneficial things were now being regularly added to a more contented Brian.

Occasionally the veteran Jeff resurfaced at the charity to refuel his alcohol wrecked metabolism with a meal then disappear back out onto the streets. On each visit Brian would ensure that a little extra tucker was put on Jeff's plate. Knowing Jeff was a man of few words Brian would generally have only a brief exchange regarding his mate's well-being. One evening Jeff lingered until it was nearly time to close. Brian noted the change in his behaviour and finished his tasks ahead of time so that he might chat with him.

Brian sensed something was definitely wrong when he sat down alongside his friend. He could hear Jeff labouring to breath.

"You're puffing a bit there mate – sounds like you're having a bit of strife breathing," Brian said to open the conversation as he slid a cup of tea towards Jeff.

"I'm not doing too well – the doctor said I have pneumonia and wanted me to stay in hospital for a few days – couldn't do that – hate being inside a building for more than a few minutes so I legged it when his back was turned."

When Brian was younger, his uncle had died from the complications of pneumonia and this sent alarm bells ringing in his thoughts.

"You can't stay outside in the cold, the bloody pneumonia will only get worse, then you're a goner," Brian said as he placed his arm around Jeff's once broad but now boney shoulders.

"Haven't got much to live for, so carking it will be no big deal," Jeff replied as he gasped for his next breath.

Brian looked Jeff in the eyes and said, "What say you come and camp with me – got a little hut to live in these-days – there'd be enough room for you too I reckon. Won't be flash but at least you'll be warm."

Jeff dropped his head and stared at the table for a few moments, "has it got a verandah, I'd feel better if I could sleep outside – might get 'closter' inside."

To which Brian replied, "How about you try inside first – I have plenty of blankets".

It was a painfully slow walk home for the pair. Jeff could only manage a few paces before stopping for a breather.

"Take your time mate – we don't have to rush off to anywhere special so there is no hurry to get home," Brian said jokingly trying to lighten the moment.

Finally, after much puffing and pausing the pair reached the cabin. In typical army blokes-talk, Brian explained to Jeff, "The latrines are at the back of the shed if you gotta go, no pissing over the verandah."

This brought a slight smile to Jeff's lips.

"What time is reveille, Sarg?" Jeff gasped.

"Unless you have another appointment with the Medic there is no rush to be on parade," Brian said as he handed Jeff a pair of blankets then flashed a quick salute at him.

"Shit, it has been a long time since anyone saluted me. If I weren't so flaming crook I would do a bit of square bashing with you – just to see if you can still keep in step," Jeff wheezed with a touch of laughter in his voice then laid on the small piece of carpet that had been donated to the charity and snaffled by Brian for the hut floor.

Throughout the night Brian would stir and listen to the rasping breaths Jeff was taking. As he lay thinking, his mind shifted on what he should do for him and to how to get any needed medication for his mate.

Eventually the mysterious peace spirit of the hut settled Brian into a deep sleep until the soft light of morning illuminated the room. Before his eyes opened Brian instinctively listened for Jeff's breathing. There was silence, no sound of his mate labouring to get a lung full of air. In panic Brian jumped out from under his covers expecting to find a body on the floor where Jeff slept and ripped back the bedding that had covered him last night.

Jeff had gone. Brian pounced to his feet and grabbed at the door handle and realised the door was now partially opened, not shut as he had left it last night. Flinging back the door in panic he looked outside. Jeff was laying on the verandah and the sickening feeling of him being dead, again made Brian shudder as he extended his arm to squeeze Jeff's shoulder. Jeff let out a moan as Brian's grip was felt.

"Christ mate you just scared the hell out of me – I thought you were fuckin' dead," Brian blurted out.

"Not dead yet – needed some open air," Jeff rasped back and struggled to sit upright.

Brian reached out to assist but Jeff brushed aside his arm. "Stand at ease soldier - I can do it" Jeff humorously rebuked Brian then followed with another laboured breath - "Got any rations?"

The two sat on the verandah in silence as they munched on some home-made fruit cake that Lou had baked. The hush was broken when Jeff laboriously coughed then flippantly quipped, "A bloke would get fat in a hurry if he ate this stuff everyday".

To which Brian replied with a slightly serious tone, "You could do with a bit more weight ya skinny bastard – your uniform would fall off you the way you are now – you wouldn't even pass a nearly blind sergeants parade inspection."

For a few minutes they sat in silent contemplation of what had just been said. Each dwelling on what to do next.

"Got nothing to live for so why bother trying to put a bit of meat on my bones," Jeff said as he looked directly at Brian.

"What about family?" Brian enquired.

"Only got a sister but haven't seen her for ages," Jeff muttered.

"I thought you told me that your father was still going – got book shops?" Brian asked.

"He disowned me when I hit the grog after coming back from the Middle East. Haven't spoken to him since - I am not the arse lickin' son he wanted so stuff him and his books," Jeff replied, and he went into a coughing spasm.

Hearing the sound of Jeff's struggle for breath and watching his coughing fit, Brian realised it was vital to take immediate action to halt his mates health from deteriorating any further.

In an officious voice Brian stated, "As the highest rank in the base I am giving you an order Corporal – you are going to attend sick parade today – got that soldier? There's a motorbike in the motor pool that we can use – the transport is organised – so let's get going."

Jeff sat shaking his head as he quietly rasped, "Pullin' rank now – s'pose I have no alternative – orders are orders."

The doctor was furious, and berated Jeff for his stupidity. "You may want to die – but that's not going to happen - I swore an oath to preserve life and you will do as I tell you – 'YOU' – whether you like it or not – 'YOU' – will stay in hospital and in bed until I say otherwise," the doctor blasted.

For the second time, the doctor admitted Jeff into hospital – But on this occasion with strict orders ensuring his patient was to be kept in until he and only he as the doctor responsible, deemed Jeff well enough for release.

Brian's daily itinerary now included a trip to the hospital. Having the motorbike was a godsend which allowed time for both the volunteer work and to visit his mate. Each day he saw a gradual increase in Jeff's health and put forward the suggestion to Jeff that it may not be too long before he would be released.

There was no reaction by Jeff to what Brian had commented about getting out. Only a vacant stare of Jeff's eyes into nowhere in particular.

"What's the matter mate – don't you want to get out into the open air again?"

Jeff lifted his head towards Brian "It has been the most days straight I have ever spent inside any building since I left home – totally forgot what a bed felt like – a bloke could get to like sleeping in one again. Maybe I should go and patch things up with the old-boy – ya never know he might even give me a job!"

Brian then looked Jeff in the eye, "Why the change of attitude? – You vowed that you would never go back and start talking to your father again."

"Nearly shit myself when I thought I was gunna die – I've realised can't croak it without making peace with me old man – it's something I have to do – so dying is out of the question now," Jeff said quietly as tears filled his eyes. "I always had hoped that my Dad would come looking for his son and rescue me from the gutter – as far as I know he never tried to find me – stubborn bastard. It seems like it is now up to me to go crawling back and ask his forgiveness."

For several minutes the two blokes just sat in silence. Each pondering the magnitude of what had just been said. Jeff dwelt on whether he would be received or booted out again. Brian thoughts drifted into being reunited with his family then broke the silence

"Yeh mate, I feel your pain – I have always wished that Suzanne would come looking for me – I can't go to her – the other baby, the new bloke would make it almost impossible for her to understand just how much I have missed them – looks like my pain will never end – but you at least now have a chance of sorting your life out."

It was almost three weeks before Jeff had been assessed as being well enough to be discharged. Brian had bought some second-hand clothes and shoes he found at an op-shop that would fit Jeff. On the day of being released the two men held a small ceremony – the disposal of Jeff's old clothing. In true army style with total disregard to the passing public outside of the hospital, the pair of ex-soldiers positioned themselves in front of a council litterbin. Standing at attention, saluted the bin then tossed in the tattered remnants of what would be the last reminders of Jeff's past few years, then stood together motionless for the mandatory minute of silence.

The confined space of the small cabin was inadequate for two men to live comfortably and definitely not a place for Jeff to be sitting alone throughout day, so Brian suggested that his convalescing mate might accompany him to the charity kitchen each day rather than moping around in the hut with little to do and become bored.

Jeff was at first reluctant to follow Brian's advice until he was convinced that getting out into the fresh air and being amongst other people would hasten his recovery. Brian's ulterior motive was to keep Jeff in his sight then could also ensure that Jeff was eating enough nourishing food.

At the charity the weakened Jeff would just sit at a table, read the newspapers, drink tea and partake of the food provided by Brian. On the days when he was feeling good, Jeff would position himself alongside the dish wash area and lend a hand to pre-clean the plates by scraping off any left-over food scraps. It was only simply task yet it gave Jeff a sense of being useful and not just a free-loader. Brian understood that when Jeff's strength fully returned and the time was right he would make the move to reunite with his father. In the meantime, keeping his mate off the grog and getting good food into him was more important than being concerned about cramped conditions back at the hut or when he will meet his old man.

Out of the blue on the third Saturday morning after his release from hospital, Jeff asked the question, "Hey Brian, Can you do me a favour mate?"

To which Brian replied with a puzzled look. "Tell me what it is you want done, then I will say yah or nay."

Jeff responded, "Can you take me on the bike into town? – I need to have a look to see if me oldie is still running the bookshop. Reckon it might be a good idea to have practice run and check out the place again. Do a bit of a 'reckie' and eyeball the codger without him knowing." Then he added in a fake joking tone, "Still shittin' me self about meeting with him again. Don't even know if the old coot is still alive – it's been friggin' years since we talked."

"I am with you all the way on this one – it's going to take a load of courage to make the first move – a different sort of bravery than fighting a mongrel enemy," Brian said as he put a reassuring arm around Jeff's shoulder.

After a quick stop into the local servo for some fuel for the BMW, Brian and Jeff headed into the city.

"Drive past first would ya mate – wanna see if the place has changed," Jeff yelled through his helmet visor as they neared the main bookshop. Brian obliged and pulled the bike into a parking space about 100 metres beyond the shop.

"The place has had a bit of a paint job since I saw it last – that was years ago – couldn't get up enough nerve to come anywhere near here. Shit-scared the old man would see me if I did," Jeff said as he took off his helmet.

"Got enough nerve to take a walk past the shop?" Brian asked as he placed his helmet over one of the bike's rear view mirrors.

"No guts no glory, so s'pose I'd better do it before I chicken out," said Jeff plonking his helmet on the other mirror stalk.

In silence the two walked towards the shop. The closer they came, Brian could hear Jeff taking deliberate long breath intakes followed by equally lengthy exhales. Jeff stopped walking for a moment then muttered 'gotta do it, gotta do it' then began walking forward again after a quick glance to check if Brian was still alongside him.

The front door was beginning to open as they drew level with the bookshop, Jeff kept on walking, noticeably staring directly ahead, but now at a slightly quicker pace until they were a few shops beyond their planned destination. He stopped and turned around and grabbed Brian's arm and stated, "Struth – that was my sister Jillian coming out the shop – what in the hell she is doing there?!"

The two men stood intentionally trying to be inconspicuous while they watched as the 'sister' remove the Now Open signboard from the footpath and carried it back inside the shop. A few moments passed before she reappeared and locked the door with a bunch of keys, crossed the road and climbed into a car parked opposite and drove away.

"Saturday – two o'clock closing," was all that Jeff said as they walked back to the store where they paused and peered through the front widow. The shelves were stacked with thousands of books with cards above each section identifying genre or author.

Back at the motorbike Brian said, "Seems the shop is still doing good business – got heaps of stock and it looks like someone is looking after the joint."

Jeff never replied to Brian's comment, he just stood looking back toward the bookshop seemingly deep in thought.

"You OK mate?" Brian asked as he reached out and placed his hand on Jeff's shoulder.

"That was an unnerving experience – never thought I would have the courage to go anywhere near the place," Jeff said softly as he rocked his head gently from side to side.

"Well you did and that's a start – maybe you might pluck up enough nerve to drop in and say hello to your sister next time – you will need to know if the old man is still kicking," Brian said as he swung his leg over the motorbike and motioned to Jeff to get on.

"Thanks mate for taking me – you helped me through the first stage – would you mind being there for me next time?" Jeff said as he positioned himself on the bike's saddle.

"That's what friends are for – hope you would do the same for me someday," Brian responded.

Life had become much the same as if the two men were living

in the close confines of a military camp. Each day fell into a pattern of regularity. First thing in the morning was a parade march to the ablution facility at the rear of Lou's garage. After that, the cabin tidied and a quick walk to the soup kitchen for breakfast. Jeff's health was improving rapidly and he had gained some much needed weight that had not gone un-noticed by Brian.

"Mate - If you keep up eating three meals a day you'll end up fatter than me – best I've ever seen you look. You must have been doing more groggin' on instead of eating," quipped Brian to which Jeff light-heartedly replied.

"The grog had a hold on me but I am staying off it now." Then he chuckled and added – "Seems you've been doing some grazing in a good pasture longer than me – best thing you ever did was to volunteer for some Dixie-bashing at the kitchen - plenty of rations each day." He paused for a moment then said in a more serious tone, "Being here with you and the volunteers to feed the other poor bastards has given me another reason for keeping off the booze. The grog nearly cost me my life and if wasn't for you, I probably would have ended up on a cold slab in a morgue somewhere – seems that helping others is a bloody good way to get yourself back on track – you know what I mean?"

Sometimes the journey through life has multiple twists and turns along its path. Often the changes that occur along the way come from the most unexpected sources.

On a sunlit but breezy morning not long after their trip to the bookshop, Brian and Jeff were lazing about reading some of the other books left inside the cabin. There was knock on the cabin door and Brian opened it to find it was Louise with a big smile on her face.

"With a grin like that it looks as if you've won the lottery," Brian said as he stepped out onto the verandah.

"Better than that," Louise replied "My son is getting married in Hawaii and I am going to the wedding – then I'm off to the States for five months. I have a cousin there who's asked me to come and stay with her. She's going to meet me at the wedding and then we'll be traveling together from Hawaii to her home in Los Angeles."

"Could you use a couple of fellows to carry your bags?" Jeff said as he poked his head out of the doorway.

"Sorry lads, only have the one suitcase – I think I can manage that," Lou giggled. Then in a more serious tone went on to say, "What I have come for is to ask if you will look after the house and keep the volunteers in line while I'm gone. You can stay in the house and use the downstairs bedrooms. It will be better for me know that someone I can trust is in the place – that way no thieves will be trying to break in and steal anything. I have seen how neat and clean you have kept the cabin so I have no doubt you will do the same in the house."

Brian looked at Jeff as if they too had won the lottery. "We would love to Lou – it was getting a bit tight in the barracks so a stint in a real house would be just like a holiday for us as well – yes, you can have a fab holiday knowing we will look after your lovely home – it would be our pleasure as you have been extra kind and generous – it is the least we can do for you."

For the first time in several years the luxury of living in a real house allowed the mental state of both men to settle and enjoy living. Brian kept the house spotless and Jeff being the more outdoors type ensured that all of Louise's potted plants and flower beds received full attention – so much so, they flourished better than they had done previously.

Saturday mornings were mainly spent reading the newspaper while the clothes were being automatically washed in Lou's latest model machine. Brian was in the laundry placing another load into the washer when Jeff called out to him.

"Hey Sergeant, you had better come and answer the door – there is a couple of Jay-Dubs knocking. If I go, I reckon they won't like me telling them to piss off - you might be a bit nicer and politely ask them to remove their religious arses from the verandah."

Brian answered the door, as Jeff had predicted, they were Jehovah Witnesses. Two clean-cut men dressed in deliberate non-fashionable freshly ironed shirts and trousers, each carrying satchels and with a copy of the Watch-tower tract in their hands ready to place at this house. "Good morning Sir, Would you have a few minutes so that we can speak of Jehovah's plan for mankind. I am Brother Raymond and this Brother William.

In Brian's pre-military service days the J.Ws had regularly knocked on his door. With polite conversation and his admission to being a Catholic plus a donation for another never-to–be-read Watchtower or Awake magazine the visitors usually vacated his front porch and moved on to their next 'victim'. Today Brian was in a different frame of mind and was curious as to the religious view point these two well-dressed men were trying to deliver. The messengers quoted scripture and supposed facts and figures of when the world as we know it will end – Armageddon as they called it. Brian simply nodded his head as if he was interested but internally saying to himself – 'Wonder how many more times this 'end-of-the-world will be predicted' but never happens.

The visitors were in full stride quoting their pre-rehearsed spiel and their confidence of converting Brian was visibly obvious. Suddenly, Brian's attention was diverted to the two neatly dressed ladies with large handbags that were unmistakably part of the 'team' door-knocking the neighbourhood. In a flash both of the JWs realised that Brian was no longer listening to their banter and stopped.

"Who is that one on the right?" Brian nervously asked.

"That is Sister Suzanne – she is new to our Kingdom Hall," Brother Raymond said with a quizzical look on his face – "I believe her husband and their youngest child were tragically killed in a motor vehicle accident recently. She came to us searching for answers in her life – do you know her?"

Instead of having to reply to his question, luckily for Brian, the washing machine's out-of-balance alarm began screeching.

"Gonna have to go, the washing machine is needing urgent attention – thanks for calling," He quickly closed the door on the two. Instead of heading toward the laundry he turned left into the living room.

"What's the matter Sarg – you look as though you've seen a ghost - Did those blokes put the fear of Christ into ya?" Jeff asked as Brian sat on the lounge edge in a visibly distraught state.

"No – bloody worse than that – just saw my ex and she's one of them. They reckon her bloke and his kid got killed in a car smash-up not long ago. Shit! That's all I needed to happen. Just when things were going so well. I wish now that you had answered the door and sent packing, then I wouldn't have seen her or known anything".

Brian sat and kept nodding his head and muttering to

himself, "Why now, why me? I thought everything was fine, then 'she' happens to reappear. I thought I was over her. Why! Why! Why! Bugger it Jeff, I am going out to the cabin so I can think things over and get the crap out of my mind – I need the space – if they come back or anyone else wants me - tell them to eff-off, will ya?"

Often magic happens in our lives but very few ever see when it unveils itself. Without any planned direction Brian had embarked on a journey through life, never really knowing what lay ahead. He simply took each day as it arrived. Some were good and some had painful lessons within them. This day he was again exposed to his past life and his reaction was not out of the ordinary. He needed to recompose his thinking and decide how he would react to this situation.

The aura of the cabin was something of an enigma. Within a few minutes an unexplainable tranquillity would envelope those that entered. Brian had often experienced the inner effect of this phenomenon. Today when the much agitated Brian came in and sat for a few moments on the cabins sofa – his entire mood took an about face and a calmness pervaded his being. His mind now seemed empty of the thoughts that plagued him moments ago when in the house. For no reason what-so-ever Brian selected the book of poems from the shelf – the same one he had read from when he first found refuge here in the cabin. Flicking through the pages his eyes caught a poem that he had previously read snippets.

"Looking for that someone – someone who will really care. Someone who will love you – no matter what you do. Someone that will be with you – to help you see things through. Someone with a quiet strength and a heart of pure gold. Some who knows your needs – never having to be told" The words leapt from the page and went deep into Brian's subconscious. "Yes -This is what I need – I need somebody that I can love and they will love me." Brian muttered to himself. His mind then shifted to thoughts of Suzanne. Is it her Karma that her bloke and child got killed – Is it payback for doing the dirty on me? Brian's emotions for her were mixed. 'Should I try to love her again or should I forget her altogether' he pondered while various scenarios of both ideas flashed through his mind. A pang of guilt about giving the children a father again brought him to the realisation there was also another child that was not his. This tot was his daughter's sister and they too would have experienced some grief by the tragedy. Understanding their loss would be difficult – perhaps even harder than re-loving Suzanne after she had dispirited his entire being. "What should I do, what can I do?" he repeated several times while trying desperately to find a solution to his thinking.

Brian lay on the sofa to mull the various possibilities then as often happened in the past, drifted into a deep sleep. It was late evening when Jeff knocked on the door yelling "Hey mate – are you OK. Got tea ready if you want to eat? – made a beef ragout with lots of vegies in it. Just about to plate it up.!" To which a sleepy Brian replied "Righto. Be there in five. Make mine a big serve – bloody hungry, thanks to those Jay dubs I missed lunch."

After consuming two plates of the stew prepared by Jeff, the satiated Brian was now in a happier frame of mind and complimented the Mess Sergeant, "Not bad grub for an old soldier – better than those ration packs we had." Then he paused for a moment then went on to say "Been thinking things over. What I need is a good woman in my life. Thought about making up with Suzanne but there would be too many ghosts in that cupboard and I am not sure if I could handle them. Don't get me wrong – deep down I sort of think I loved her... but – I'm not sure whether it was real love. Probably just infatuated with her. Reckon I would be better off not going back, I have to start again. All I need to do now is meet someone else, preferably a lovely hearted woman that has no baggage."

"Best of luck mate," Jeff replied as he wiped a piece of bread through the last remnant of gravy on his plate. "That was bloody good tucker – my compliments to me."

With a mouth still half full with bread he carried on the conversation. "Brian, hope you haven't forgotten that I have to go and face the music or should I say books. We had better get that over and done with before you race off searching for a new lady in your life. What say we make it next week sometime, eh – Mate?"

To which Brian replied "Weather permitting and if the motorbike starts we could do it," then sat deep in thought about what type of woman he would choose. Totally ignoring Jeff's request to help do a bit of Dixie-bashing with the plates and pans.

It was now two months since Lou went to America. Heavy rain throughout the week halted any visit to the bookshop. Both men spent much of their daylight and evening hours working in the kitchen of the charity trying to keep up with the wet-weather induced higher demand for food for the homeless. For the time being Brian's thoughts of finding a new woman were put on hold and Jeff's bookshop visit was also placed on the back burner.

On the following Saturday the weather had cleared.

"Do think we should take a run to your Dad's book store this morning," Brian said as he stuffed a week's worth of soiled clothes into the washing machine.

"I'm game if you are," Jeff replied then added, "Better make it there before the place closes at two. Fifteen minutes before that – would be enough for me to meet the old enemy then I've got the excuse of closing time to make an escape if needed."

"Clever tactics – hit and run," replied Brian.

The sun was warm and the air was sweetly freshened after the previous days of rain. Ideal for motorbike riding. Apart from a few nuisance red traffic light stops the two made good time getting to the bookshop as planned.

"Want me to come in with you?" Brian asked as Jeff handed his helmet to him.

"No thanks mate - I might be shaking in my socks but I have to do this mission on my own. You keep out here as backup and stay with the bike for a quick retreat – just in case any shit hits the fan," Jeff said as he drew a deep breath and headed towards the store.

Jeff bravely approached the bookstore, hesitated for a moment outside the door where he took another lung full of air, then cautiously entered the building.

Meanwhile Brian sat patiently on the motorbike awaiting his mates return. Being a Saturday afternoon much of the traffic had dispersed from the street with only a few vehicles now occupying the curbside parking spaces. Brian's eyes were drawn to a vintage Morris Minor parked directly opposite the bookshop. He was able to see that someone was sitting in the driver's seat. Only having their back of head in view he was unable to determine their age or gender and paid little further attention to the vehicle and its occupant.

The minutes ticked by and Brian became restless just sitting around waiting for Jeff. With the thought in mind that Jeff's family had no idea that Jeff and he were mates, Brian realised that he could venture closer to the shop and not be recognised and have a look. As he neared the premise he saw the person in the Morris alight from the vehicle. She was indeed a rather attractive young woman. Not a bad sort of lady, neatly dressed, no visible tattoos, and the added bonus of having a very nice figure, he mentally noted. His thoughts were suddenly halted as she walked directly toward him. Averting his gaze from her he turned his head and pretended to be looking through the shop window. The woman's path then veered a little taking her to the store door. Through the glass Brian could see Jeff talking to what he assumed was the sister. It also appeared evident that Jeff's father was not in the store. Sighting the arrival of the woman, Jeff's sister held out her arms to her and gave a welcoming hug. Brian could gather by their actions the sister was then introducing Jeff to the woman and then a similar welcome hug followed for him.

All three seemed to be comfortable with each other's presence. Brian felt tempted to go inside. Not being invited in he opted to stay outdoors. Jeff then sighted Brian standing outside and beckoned for him to also enter. Sheepishly Brian stepped into the store. Once inside the combination of fresh ink of newly printed best sellers and the peppery aroma that seeped from between the covers of antiquarian volumes written by past authors confirmed to his senses that the shop had been trading there for many years.

"Sis, this is the bloke I was telling you about – Brian - the best mate a fellow could have. Brian this is my sister Jillian and this young lady is her long-time friend, Cheryl," Jeff said as he walked over to and stood beside Brian.

A flush of red washed over Brian's cheeks. Just minutes before he was noting the 'physical qualities' of the woman and within a moment or two, was being introduced to her.

"Hello Brian," Cheryl said as she put forward her hand forward ready to accept a handshake. "Pleased to meet you" she said as Brian reciprocated. Their hands lingered together for a moment or two. When Brian realised it was Cheryl still holding his, it caused his pulse to quicken.

"N-nice to meet you," he nervously in reply just a she slowly released her gentle grip.

Jeff and Jillian were engrossed in conversation of the many events that had occurred over the years that Jeff was AWOL from his family. Cheryl and Brian were virtually left to make their own conversation. Basic cordialities were exchange and a few questions and answers regarding how long each other had been acquainted. Cheryl had been a high-school friend of Jill's and had remained close friends, often meeting for coffee or going shopping together. For Brian it was a tad awkward to explain meeting Jeff when they were both down and outs. Instead of the truth, Brian white-lied a little and lead Cheryl to believe they had met through their involvement in the armed forces.

The conversations continued for a few minutes, until a customer entering the shop questioned Jill regarding what time the shop shuts.

"The sign outside says two o'clock," stated the customer.

"Actually we do close at two but I forgot to bring in the sign," Jill hurriedly said as she brushed past the shopper to retrieve the 'Now Open' metal signboard.

Jeff took advantage of the interruption and motioned to Brian that they should be leaving. Jillian offered for her brother to meet one evening for a meal. She suggested next Friday fortnight. Saying this would give her time to include their father. This halted Jeff in his tracks.

"Not sure if I can make it then," replied a rather startled brother.

But Brian spudded in, "Yes he can – I'll make sure he does, just give me a call on this number to confirm what time and where," he said as he pulled a piece of paper from his pocket with Louise's home phone number and handed it to her. He then gave a polite "goodbye - nice to meet you" to Cheryl as both men exited the store.

"What in the hell did you do that for," Jeff exploded Brian as they prepared to don their motorcycle helmets. "I am not ready to see the old fart just yet – still shaking from meeting my sister."

"No good retreating while you are mid battle. You have to keep on with the operation and reach your objective. Seeing your father again wasn't it?" Brian reminded his mate.

On the trip home neither spoke a word. Each in their own world taking in the events of the book-store mission. Brian's thoughts centred entirely on how lovely was Cheryl and what made his heart raced at the mere touch of her hand.

Now that he had recuperated to a level of fitness normality, Jeff was also working a full day at the Charity. Brian had suggested that Jeff might get work with his sister at the bookstore.

"Not ready yet," came a quick answer from Jeff. "Have to pay them back for all the free food I've eaten here and I still need to be reminded of what living in the gutter means. Every day I see others in the same position I had been and how far I had fallen out of society. I really do not want to end up living rough again."

Brian smiled at his mate and said, "I know what you mean, that's why I am still here doing my bit to help."

On the Wednesday evening, after the visit to the bookstore, Jillian phoned Lou's number. Being closest to the phone Brian answered. The call was to let Jeff know the time and place for the dinner date with her and Dad. She had chosen a quiet restaurant not far from the store. One that she often went to with Cheryl and some other friends.

"Would you like to come too?" she asked Brian.

"Thanks, but no," he replied. "It is a family affair, however I will make sure Jeff gets there on time. I can sit back here at home and if needed all he has to do is phone and I will come and collect him."

Jeff's previous happy demeanour change the instant Brian related the time to be at the restaurant.

"Nearly every day it appears I have to face another test and Friday I get the big one," Jeff muttered.

"Don't think you're an orphan, I have had heaps of personal tests mate," Brian responded. "Seems like I was never aware of what happens around me until I started changing my thinking and the way I live. Years ago my Grandpa would tell me that the two things go hand in hand. Change your inner thoughts and a stack of tests appear out of no-where. If you pass one trial, another crops up out of the blue. Some might call it character building – I call it a flamin' nuisance but if it makes me a better bloke, I will have to accept all the shit thrown at me, so will you."

As the two men were about to leave for the dinner meeting

with Dad and sister, Brian said "I'll drop you off at the restaurant and hightail it back here. If you need a lift home again, just call me," then beckoned for Jeff to get on the bike. He gave the motor a few rev's, clicked the foot lever into first gear and headed out the driveway.

It wasn't long before Brian eased off the throttle, dropped back down through the gears and pulled the motorbike into a parking space in the venue carpark.

"Stay calm and enjoy the night and remember to keep your mouth shut about us being a couple of ex street bums. They don't need to know," Brian said as Jeff attached his helmet to the carrier clip. "Only talk about working at the Charity or being sick. Leave out the grog part and when you were living rough," he went on to say, then shook Jeff's hand firmly as a gesture of true mateship.

Brian sat and watched Jeff approach the front door and enter the restaurant. He was about to kick-start the BMW he saw an old chap in a wheel chair being guided by a woman going into the same place. A thought flashed across his mind, 'Wonder if it was the Dad – nah! Probably just some other old geezer, Jill had said nothing about their Dad being in a chair.'

He then fired up the bike a headed back home.

Sitting watching television became monotonous as he waited for the call to fetch Jeff. Brian needed to find something more stimulating, so he meandered over to Louise's bookshelf. Running his fingers across the spines he scanned the titles for one that may be of interest to read. No particular book caught his attention until his slow hand sweep halted on 'Getting more out of your life' by George R Williams. After sliding the book out of the shelf Brian retreated to the comfort of an armchair and began reading.

He thought the preamble was a bit boring – all about some bloke that came out from England with his family. Then chapter one revealed how the young fellow did it tough when he left home against his parent's wishes. The author described how he worked on a farm miles from any town. The scorching summer heat, the dust, flies and snakes were totally opposite to the lush green hedge enclosed grassy pastures of England where butterflies and robins flittered in the warm sunshine.

The next few paragraphs focused on how the chap portrayed, endured the character building struggle of life without parental support. What Brian was reading appeared to have nothing to do with 'Getting more' but mostly about the hardship of a bloke's life. His curiosity urged him to skip a chapter or two in an effort to find something more about what the title inferred.

When he finally settled to read a random selected chapter, the storyline became more interesting, especially where the author gave insight into how the mind forms subconscious habits, or as described, the way the brain operates using 'Neuron Pathways or Tracks' formed during our life. He wrote, "The lack of parental love and those hardships endured by the young Englishman in the first chapter would set long-term reactive behaviour in his brain. These embedded 'Pathways of Brain Activity' can lead people to disregard the desire to seek alternative options. They continue to live in unhappy situations rather than create for themselves a better life. Neuron tracks require re-routing if one's life is to change. Two examples the writer illustrated – persons that habitually watch a TV soap series most days at the same time over several years have an embedded neuron path. People that live in a loveless relationship who only stay because of a fear of being alone. Such daily routines form the pathways of brain activity that become entrenched as a constant behaviour pattern.

Brian said to himself as he bookmarked the page for future reading. "Not me – hate those fake reality shows." Then he realised, "I may still have some pathways that formed when I was younger. I can understand the loveless part. Perhaps I need to make some changes in my life."

"Time for cuppa," he mumbled as he rose from his seat. As he did, the phone rang. "Good timing Jeff – just about to make a cuppa and now you want me to come and get you." Brian said without waiting for the caller to identify themselves.

"Wrong on both counts," came the voice of Jillian, "Cheryl has turned up at the restaurant and she will drive my brother back again, I have to take Dad back home – by the way everything went well and we had a great night – see you another time," then she hung up before Brian could say anything.

The sound of a motor vehicle pulling into the driveway had Brian heading for the front door. As he opened the house door, Jeff was alighting from Cheryl's old Morris.

"Can't stop now Brian, will catch up with you soon," she called out from the car, then reversed the little vehicle out to the road. All Brian could do was give her a wave as she drove away.

"You made it back in one piece – no hidden roadside bombs got you then," Brian quipped to his mate as they entered the house.

Once inside, Jeff said, "I did get hit by one exploding grenade – didn't see that one coming!"

"What do you mean?" Brian enquired. "The old fart is in a

wheel chair and living in a nursing home," Jeff said as he wiped his hand down past his eyes then held his chin and jaw and ponder the long-overdue meeting. "Tonight has knocked the stuffing out of me – let you know all about tomorrow – I'm heading for bed," Jeff said as he aimed his body towards his bedroom.

Next day, Jeff re-counted the previous evening. The shock of seeing his father in a wheel chair had almost bought him to tears. However when his Dad said how much he missed his son and the countless times he had thoughts of him, it gave the tear ducts the little nudge that released many years of pent-up emotion in both men. With tears flowing, on wobbly legs his father managed to stand long enough for his son to give him a much needed and loving hug.

From that point onwards the lost years of the past evaporated. Jeff described to Brian how he and his father sat together after the meal holding each other's hand reminiscing of many things they had done together prior to him donning a uniform and heading off to the Middle East. Hearing Jeff describe his reconciling with his father sent stabbing pangs of emotion through Brian's heart. The need for resolution with his family grew in his thoughts. Then the voice of 'it's all too late' quashed his thinking in that arena. Despite the mind chatter Brian knew in his heart that one day he would need to meet with his ex and daughters to at least attempt of reconciling with them.

Jeff's outlook on life was now enriched. The bogies of the past were in-part buried and the new bonding with his family dispersed much of his negativity. A few weeks after the reunion Jeff literally waltzed up to Brian and proudly stated, "You know mate, miracles do bloody happen. My sister and Cheryl hope to go on a cruise around the Pacific Islands and guess what? – She wants me to look after the shop! Do you suppose you can run the charity kitchen without me? Louise will probably be back by then, what do you think eh! Do you reckon I would be up to the task?"

A big smile filled Brian's face. "Up to it! You'd be a bloody natural at selling stuff - I've seen how you talk to the poor buggers coming in for a meal and giving them advice. Books will be easy-peasy. All you will have to do is remember who wrote what and you have got it made. One problem! How will you get back and forth, I won't be able to take you on the bike everyday cos it will clash with the times I have to be at the soup shop."

"No problemo" Jeff replied, "There's a flat at the back of the shop where Dad stayed when he worked late."

The change in his mate was obvious. Jeff had gained weight and was abstaining from the grog. Brian felt a tad envious then he took stock of the nicer points that were happening in his life. Many of the good things were the result of Lou's kindness. A sudden revelation occurred in his thoughts. Much that has happened has been directly linked to Louise. The cabin, the job, the BMW, staying in the house, seeing his ex, his mateship with Jeff, all connected with this remarkable lady. Everything pointed to some inexplicable reason or maybe there actually was a spiritual connection. His thoughts then turned to the calming effect of the cabin and the role it was playing in his journey. The words of the poem that he had read in the hut repeated themselves in his mind. 'Along life's path we travel, never knowing what each day will bring. Brian nodded his head in agreeance and repeated the words over again in his mind then spoke them out aloud several times, as if he was memorising them for an oral exam. Then the question filled his thinking– 'Why Louise? Why the cabin? Why me?'

A postcard sent by Louise from America arrived at the Charity Kitchen with just a few words quickly penned on the back. "Hello everyone – hope all is good. Will be home in a couple of weeks. Tell you all about my trip when I get there. Love to you all, Lou."

Working each day and looking after Lou's house and plants gave Brian no time to socialise. On an impulse Friday night he reneged having a meal at the charity kitchen or bothering to cook dinner at home. "Tonight I will treat myself to a meal at a café," he announced to himself. Then uttered the question "Which one?" and rummaged around to find the local newspaper to study the adverts and find a suitable venue. "Chinese, French, Japanese, Italian, mmmm Italian sounds good," and noted the address.

The host of Casa Mama met Brian as he entered the dining room and asked in an Italian accent. "Table for one or two?"

"Just the one thanks," Brian responded, and was guided to a small table adjacent to the salad bar.

For a minute or two Brian sat and surveyed the room soaking up the pleasure of being in a restaurant. Haven't had chef cooked nosh up for years, in fact it has been ages since I dined out he thought as he perused the menu, finally deciding on the ethnically named 'Lasagne Milano'.

The service was quicker than anticipated, his meal arrived before he had time to visit the self-serve salad bar. A wonderful selection of fresh produce filled the trays in the bar. Tomato, onion, olives and an egg-plant cold combination he spooned onto his plate, while listening to the backdrop of soft Italian music.

As he was about to replace the serving tongs into the tray a woman's voice probed, "Haven't seen you here before, Brian." This startled him slightly as he had not anticipated he would be recognised by anyone with whom he was acquainted.

Turning around he saw Cheryl and another woman standing behind him.

"Thought I would give myself a treat and have someone cook for me tonight – it was overdue – need to get out more," he rattled off as if he were a rabbit caught in the bright beam of a spotlight.

"Care to join us - we haven't ordered yet," Cheryl asked as she heaped a pile of garden salad onto a plate.

"Th-Thanks for asking, my meal is already served and going cold, it would be rude of me to be eating in front of you," he responded jitterily.

"What about taking a rain-check and catching up with each other next time you do not feel like cooking?" replied Cheryl.

"That would be nice," Brian said, nodding his head in agreeance then returned to his table.

Back home Brian reminisced how dining out was indeed a rare treat for him. The pasta was cooked to perfection with the true Italian flavours he loved. The daily grind of being in a crowded soup kitchen certainly lacked the atmosphere of having an actual restaurant experience. Small pangs of yearning for more of the same jabbed at his mind as he recollected the days when Suzanne and he were courting and eating out on weekends. For a moment Brian's thoughts drifted to watching Cheryl cross the road at the bookshop. 'Hope she does take me up that rain check,' he mused as a mental image of her cute posterior flashed across his mind.

The next two weeks rushed by and before he realised, it was time for Louise to return. Her sudden appearance at the front door caught Brian off guard. He had planned that Jeff would also be there to greet Lou back from her US holiday. The joy of seeing each other again was fully expressed in the lingering hugs they gave.

"Glad to be home again," said Lou gleefully smiling. "It was lovely staying with my cousin. She is a delightful person 'but', the amount of food they eat over there would have me fattened and ready for market if I stayed any longer. Where is Jeff?" she asked.

Brian described to her how Jeff raised the courage to visit the shop and the events that happen since then.

"Good for him, I hope he does well and finally settles down to what could be deemed a normal life once again. How have you been whilst I was abroad?" Lou asked as she settled herself on her favourite lounge. Then added, "What say we have a nice Aussie cup of tea, not coffee like in the US, and you can fill me in on all the gossip from the Charity and what you have been up to."

Over the tea Brian related how he had been helping Jeff and his quest to reconcile with his family. Lou then spotted the book Brian had been reading and followed with the question, "Did you get anything out of reading that book?" to which he replied in the affirmative. Brian then picked up the book and explained to Louise how he had an eerie sensation that lifted the words from the pages and spoke directly to him. Much the same as the one in the cabin had done.

"Seems my Roy is telling you something," Lou said as she

patted Brian's knee. "Roy wrote that book and the others that are in the cabin."

"You mean, your Roy and GRW are the one person?" Brian said with a bewildered look on his face.

"Yes," said Lou. "His full name was George Royston Williams – GRW – everyone only ever knew him as Roy." She sat in silence for a moment reminiscing about somewhere in her past and being with her now deceased soulmate. "What say we go outside and see how the garden has fared without me?" Lou offered after sipping the last drop of tea from her cup.

"Tell me more about your Roy," Brian said as they walked around, inspecting the garden area.

"The pot plants look beautiful – I think that is the best they have ever looked, was it yours or Jeff's efforts?" Lou humorously quipped as she touched the frond of a large-leafed Philodendron.

"It is all Jeff's work not mine, except for the past week or so, since he went to look after the shop," Brian said as he waited for a reply to his question about Roy.

"Let's go and sit on the garden bench in the shade and I'll tell you all about Roy." Louise said then walked towards a preferred seating spot out of the direct sun.

"Roy was a beautiful and caring man – a naturally gentle person. He was born in England, then with his parents and his older sister immigrated to Australia. Unfortunately for him both parents lived by the strict Victorian morality principle of 'Children were only to be seen, not heard'. They lacked in the affection department for their offspring. Instead, were focused on achievement and rules rather than bestowing love on their young. Feeling unloved and unable to attain the high grades they insisted he achieve, Roy left home at 14. This was contrary to their desire for him to continue with his education and 'make something of himself'. Perhaps become a banker or a lawyer. Little did they realise a young man needs to be cherished and not just an object of their social standing. Shall I keep going?" Lou then asked.

"Please do," replied Brian.

Lou continued. "For the next few years Roy accepted any job that came along. From mucking out horse stables to delivering milk. World War Two broke out, just before his eighteenth birthday. Roy took the opportunity and enlisted in the armed forces as a field ambulance driver. After doing his basic army training and completing the necessary first-aid medical education he was posted to one of the islands off Papua - New Guinea. The islands inaccessibility was a major problem for the troops and the place being vulnerable to air strikes from Japanese planes. If anyone were injured, help from a medic was limited to rudimentary first aid. The islands base hospital was only a couple of tents with a minimal range of medical equipment. The more seriously patients would be transferred to a hospital ship, sometimes the vessel might be days away."

Lou paused for a moment and recomposed herself before describing more of Roy's life.

Her voice quivered as she began, "One afternoon, several Japanese fighter planes did a surprise attack on the island. Many men were injured, some killed and an ill-fated few had limbs blown off. It was also Roy's duty to attend to these poor chaps. Stopping the bleeding with bandages and tourniquets was the best he could do. One young fellow had his right arm severed midway between the elbow and shoulder. Roy had no idea who the soldier was – his attention was focused on stemming the blood flow from the poor chap's mangled arm, then rush him back to the base in the ambulance. Time after time the planes dive bombed the island. Each time dropping explosives that made it a struggle for Roy to shift the lad out of harm's way. Fortunately, the air-raid lasted only fifteen minutes, then the Jap planes disappeared into the clouds. Roy described it as being a cowardly hit and run attack designed to create havoc and inflict as much human injuries as possible."

Images of fighting and wounded men in Afghanistan rocketed through Brian's mind as he tried to remain focused on Lou's reminiscences of her husband.

Noticing his drifting attention Lou asked, "Would you like me to stop for a while?" To which Brian answered, "Please go on," and she continued her tale.

"Back at the hospital Roy and the other first aiders acted as nurses and did whatever they could to save lives. Another of their tasks was to try and positively identify and record each patient and those that had been killed. Roy needed to fossick around in their blood soaked pockets to remove the contents then wipe it clean and place that in a bag with their ID tags. Not a nice job, especially when whatever was there was covered in all sorts of body fluids. Hope this not too gory for you to hear," she said, then added, "I suppose you saw some of the same when you were in action?"

Brian said nothing – just nodded in agreeance with her as the memory of seeing his platoon mates dying, again bolted across his mind.

Then Lou continued, "The young fellow that had half his arm blown off was not dead. He needed to be urgently evacuated. It was Roy's task to have all his paper work ready for the ship-out. The lads blood soaked clothes had been removed and were replaced with a hospital robe. Roy pulled out whatever he could find in the soldiers uniform. One item was a photo in a small folder. The outside was bloodied, the picture inside was a little worse-for-wear but still clean."

Lou reached over and held Brian's hand. "Now this is the interesting bit. Roy nearly fainted when he saw it was a picture of his sister Helen who he had not seen for many years. As a teenager she had gotten pregnant. Their parents then disowned her and had literally thrown her out of the house. Being pregnant out of wedlock bought shame on the family was their reasoning. No one ever knew what happened to her and her baby. It was there on an island in the middle of the ocean, as the result of an air-raid that Roy had found his only nephew.

"From that day forth, Roy vowed to make the world a better place and help those in need. Not only was he a caring fellow, he was also an astute business man. Much of his wealth was made through buying struggling companies that were going broke then rebuilding the business, bringing them back to making a profit then selling them again. He always strived to keep as many workers as possible in a job – that was how he did things. Much of the money he amassed went to charities. It was through Roy's generosity that our charity kitchen became a reality. That's why I give as much of my time as possible to the place – to carry on his good work and hopefully make a contribution to those in need."

"It's now quite chilly. Perhaps we should go inside," Lou said rising from her seat. A nice hot cuppa will warm us up." Then she added, "Gee, it's so nice to have a good cuppa – those Americans had no idea how to make a decent pot – coffee yes, tea no," she quipped. "Might check the mailbox first," she said and disappeared down the driveway.

Brian remained seated absorbing the tranquillity and

leafiness of the garden. Lou's recollections of her husband rekindled images of being in Afghanistan. This verdant haven was in stark contrast to the dust and barrenness of the desert. For a while he sat reflecting on being under attack and the magnitude of carnage that was inflicted on his fellow soldiers. Brian closed his eyes as few tears of compassion for Roy trickled down his face. He pictured him looking at the photo of the young man's mother – his sister. Then a pang of remorse stabbed at his heart when he realised he had neither pictures of his own sister nor any of his children or Suzanne. A feeling of being isolated from family sent a sickening wave through his innards. Brian's heart felt leaden as he wiped his cheek with the palm of his hand then drew several long deep breaths to recompose himself.

"Tea is almost ready," called Lou to encourage Brian to come inside. Within a few minutes the tea was made and poured. Both now sat at the table sipping the hot brew. "I wish you could have met my Roy, I am sure you would have become great mates," Lou said as she lifted a biscuit from the plate she had placed on the table. "You have often said that the cabin has a mystique when inside, you feel serenity there."

Brian agreed with a nod of his head as Lou nudged the platter of biscuits closer towards him. "Roy said much the same thing – what it is we will never know, but it is certainly there. In that cabin is where he did his writing. Sometimes he would forget about time and be carried away for many hours working on his next book. Occasionally I would find him sound asleep on the sofa."

Lou glanced skywards for a moment then sighed and continued her story. "If it wasn't for Roy's efforts his young nephew - David was his name - would have never made it back home alive. Would have died from the huge blood loss had a tourniquet not been quickly applied. I suppose you are wondering what ever happened to David?" Lou paused again, turned her head and looked at the photo of her husband that was on a nearby cupboard. "It was not until many months after the war had ended that Roy was able to trace the lad. Finding him also led Roy to his long lost sister." She pointed towards another picture on the shelf. "That's her standing next to Roy. Seeing each other again was a very emotional time for them. Especially for Helen. The army never told her who saved her son and now it had been revealed that her own brother was his saviour."

Grandpa's words of the guardian angel echoed in Brian's thoughts as Lou continued her story.

"After Dave was discharged from the hospital it was imperative to learn to write again. He was right handed. With that arm half gone he had no option but to use the left – for everything. Roy taught him to form letters in order to write fluently 'cacky-handed'. Lou pointed her finger indicating where the lad's limb had been severed. "The unfortunate fellow was traumatized from the incident and needed heaps of emotional support." Lou rose from her seat and took a picture of David from the shelf, looked at it for a moment, held it to her chest and sighed, then returned the photo to its original position. "I have other photos in my room, I'll go and get them," she said on the spur-of-the-moment and headed that way.

Brian went to the shelf to closer inspect the lad in the photograph. A twinge of nausea churned in his stomach on seeing the boy's long shirt sleeve cuff neatly pinned above the missing section of his arm. 'That might have been me. I could have lost a limb, or gone home in a wheelchair or worse still in a body bag like the Lance Corporal did fighting against the Taliban. Then a wince of concern flashed across his mind. Had the lad suffered the same psychological damage as he himself experienced?

Brian stared at the picture. His thoughts meandered through the ways he hid the mental trauma he endured from his family and whilst deployed in Afghanistan. Brian nodded his head in assent toward the image of the lad and said quietly to him, "I know how you feel mate, war does one's head in and defrauds us of the life we once had".

"Talking to photo's now?" Lou said as she re-entered the room somewhat flustered. "Can't seem to lay my hands on them, will try to find them some other time," she puffed.

Brian smiled with relief as the thought of ploughing through old family photos would have certainly tested his patience.

"Had enough yet? Hope I haven't been boring you," Louise ironically quipped as she sat back in her chair.

"Bit more won't hurt," Brian politely suggested.

Lou took a deep breath and continued. "Times have changed. In those days we only had type-writers. Now we have computers. Roy had a dislike for typing, his manuscripts were hand written using his favourite gold fountain pen. The pen was a gift from grateful workers in factory that he saved from bankruptcy." A smile began to glow on Lou's face. Then she hesitated prior to asking Brian, "Can you keep a secret?" Before he could offer an answer she whispered, "At his funeral viewing, I slipped that pen in the top pocket of his jacket." Then with a girlish giggle whispered, "In case he wanted to do more writing.

"Tell me to stop if you think I am just rambling on," Lou said and waited for his reply.

Brian gave Lou the thumbs up sign, "Please tell me more," he replied.

"Ok then," said Lou, then went on with her account describing Roy as a remarkable rare breed of person who had a compassion for helping those struggling. "Apart from two volumes of poetry, most of the books authored by him have a theme of overcoming difficulties, in life, love and business. Roy had a gift of entering the mind of the reader. Thousands of copies of each title were sold. That made him even richer, the more money he made the further he continued to donate".

Lou's raised hand proudly did a circular sweep of the room prior to continuing her summary of her hero. " We have this beautiful house in a quiet part of town. It was Roy's theory that when you find peace and you are with the one you love, living in place you can call home, then you have everything. Often he would remind me that money is worthless if you don't do something with it. We were in love every minute of every day – we were true soulmates - I miss him so much." Lou then sat without speaking for the next few minutes, a silence that Brian respected.

"Perhaps we should take a break now," Lou valiantly spouted out as she rose weepy-eyed from the table and headed for the kitchen. "What say I cook up something for tea?" she said, trying to discreetly wipe the tears that had begun to roll down her cheek.

"I'm not over hungry, something simple would be nice," Brian replied, then wandered out into the garden to give Lou a few moments to recompose herself.

The afternoon shadows were lengthening across the yard and the garden bench was the only place that the now feeble sun still shone. As Brian sat oblivious to the chilled air, his mind repeated the words 'in love and soulmate'.

"One day I might find my soulmate," he mused, then drifted into contemplating those that benefitted by Roy's generosity, especially the homeless like he and Jeff once were.

Ten minutes passed before Lou chirped from the verandah in a much happier tone, "Found one of your pizzas in the freezer, what say I pop that in the oven for our meal?"

"If you like, after that, I could tell you more about Roy, or you might rather fill in some of the pieces I don't know about your life," she added.

"I would prefer to hear more about Roy – but only if it's not going to upset you," Brian politely replied.

"Righty'o, pizza it is and a bit more of Roy for after's" said Lou as she went back inside.

Timely intervention by others is another of life's many mysteries. One may ponder if the arrival of someone unexpected is divine intervention or merely a coincidence, or is it?

The front door bell rang as the last pieces of pizza had been consumed. Standing at the door was Jeff and his sister Jill. "Heard you were back, Lou," Jeff said. He gave Lou a big hug as he entered the house and after a brief chat with Lou about her big trip he went on to tell the news of how he was now running the bookstore.

Jeff then relayed how he went to see their Dad. "He told me how he had sold the other shops and was holding onto this one in the vain hope that I would come back and manage the business. My sister was minding the store after father had suffered a stroke. The paralysis from the stroke put him in the wheelchair. Because I had never tried to contact my family, neither of them had any knowledge of how to find me."

Jeff stopped for a moment as a wry smile crossed his face, then continued, "Crazy how things work out. My life was on a journey of change after meeting Brian. The goodwill kitchen, becoming ill and Brian bringing me back to Lou's cabin, getting off the grog and the way things panned out after that. I reckon I must have an angel watching over me." He paused again and placed his arm around Lou, looked her in the eyes and said: "Maybe there are angels out there. One thing is for sure, we have an angel right here among us – This wonderful lady, Louise," then hugged her again.

"Thank you Jeff it's nice to be appreciated," Lou gave him a quick peck on his cheek then held his hand, "Strange as it may seem I totally agree with you. We all have someone looking after us. I often sense there are events that I can only assume are guided by my Roy. Brian and you are examples of the Roy factor. How you ended up here at my house will always remain a mystery. I can see more good things will happen for both of you. I will never stop believing that Roy's spirit is in the great somewhere continuing to do the wonderful deeds he did whilst he was alive."

She let go Jeff's hand, fumbled in her pocket and pulled out a small handkerchief and dabbed her emotionally tired eyes.

An awkward hush prevailed until Jill broke the silence, "Brian, Cheryl has met a bloke that knew you in Afghanistan and asked about catching up. I think she said his name was Colin. Would it be better for him to phone here or meet you at the charity?"

"Not sure who the Colin is? Perhaps it might be better for him to phone here one evening," Brian replied as he tried to remember the chap.

With Lou back home the daily necessity to attend the charity was lifted from Brian. He was now able to take an occasional ride on the BMW. On Sunday afternoon, as he was returning from a ride he spotted what looked like group of satchel carrying 'Jay-Dubs' a few houses down from Lou's home doing their door to door religious canvassing. Being unable to ascertain if they had already called at her place made him feel uncomfortable with the thought that Suzanne may be with them. With the bike now parked in the shed he walked to the front of the driveway and positioned himself among the branches of the shrubbery and waited to see the direction the Watchtower peddlers were heading. He breathed a sigh of relief when they continued walking away from Lou's. At that moment his emotions took another wallop when the thought of not really wanting to see his ex-wife again crossed his mind. A pang of guilt when his feelings for Cheryl over-rode those of the desire for his former love.

Instead of going into the house to see Louise, Brian trundled back to the cabin to seek answers to the many thoughts he was having. Where to from here and what would be the better direction for his life to go? His mind shuffled between making amends with his former wife and daughters, and starting life afresh with a new partner, perhaps Cheryl. No longer was he a partaker of impulsive actions. Brian had grown in compassion for other people and was aware that his life was about to take a new direction. Now the need to be considerate to those around him, including Suzanne was vital. The answer to his question was not immediately forthcoming. He lay on the sofa hugging the cushion as he reviewed his options then, once again in the unique tranquility of the cabin drifted into a deep sleep.

As the new dawn appeared Brian awoke to the melodious songs of birds in the surrounding trees. He lay listening whilst pondering an answer to solve the perplexities in his current situation. His mind remained blank except for the simple phrase 'Go with the flow and deal with each day as it happens". This puzzled him because he had no precise direction to follow. "Go with the flow, go with the flow", he muttered several times to himself until a flash of thought replaced this utterance. "Perhaps the spirit of Roy has given up on me. Now I am to work things out for myself. The only option is - to go with the flow."

He was snapped back into action when he heard Lou knocking on the cabin door and calling, "Are you awake Brian? – Jeff is on the house phone wanting to talk with you."

"Be there in a moment," Brian replied as he headed for the door. He opened it and saw Lou still in her dressing gown and appearing a tad agitated for having had to get out of bed at such an early hour. "He wouldn't ring unless it was something urgent," Lou puffed as the pair walked briskly towards the house.

"What the matter mate," Brian quizzed Jeff.

"Dad's in a bad way. My sister is away interstate and can't get back until Thursday, can you come and watch the bookshop this morning for a while so I can go to see the old fart before he carks it?" Jeff added "The electrician is coming in the morning to fit a new illuminated sign and I need someone in the shop while he's working."

"Haven't had a shower or anything to eat yet," Brian replied into the phone.

"You don't have to be there until 9.30 so you've still got plenty of time to have ya brekky. I'll wait for you so you can get in – just don't fall off your bike getting here," Jeff responded.

Jeff was standing outside the store when Brian pulled the BMW alongside the kerb. "Thanks Sarg, Cheryl is coming to pick me up," he said as he passed the set of keys to Brian then added, "Sorry to put your day out of whack but Dad had a bad night and the nurses are worried he may not see tomorrow."

As the pair entered the shop Brian reminded Jeff, "That's what mates are for – to help each other when needed. You'd better give me a quick run-down of what I'm to do so I don't look like a complete nerd."

'Go with the flow flashed across Brian's mind' as Jeff pointed out the various tasks that needed to be done throughout the day.

"Here is a number if you get into strife," Jeff said as he scribbled on a piece of paper. Brian was not paying full attention to the last few words. His eyes were fixated on the front window and looking out hoping to get a glance of Cheryl in her Morris Minor.

Jeff was rushing about like a proverbial blue-arse fly. He stacked several boxes of books on the counter until the beep-beep of the Morris horn was heard outside. Unluckily for Brian Cheryl's face was obscured by the door pillar, he was only able to see her hand waving goodbye as she and Jeff drove away.

The electrician arrived at the appointed time and began the task of installing the new sign. In the meantime Brian followed Jeff's instructions by putting away the books that had recently arrived. Throughout the day a modest number of customers came into the shop, many of whom were simply browsing in the store without making a purchase. This made the 'never sold a book before' Brian's task a lot simpler. Only a few awkward questions were asked regarding the location of various titles and Brian managed to bluff his way through with seemingly intelligent answers.

Around three o'clock the store's phone rang. It was Jeff saying that his father was still poorly and had requested that he remain with him overnight. Rather than closing the shop, Jeff asked Brian if he would be extend his favour and run the store for the next few days. He gave Brian the option to stay in the flat at the rear of the premises instead of having to travel back and forth. "There's some tucker in the fridge if you want to cook yourself a meal – and lots of icecream in the freezer. You won't go hungry," Jeff laughingly quipped.

"Had better check with Louise if the soup kitchen can do without me for another day or two - will let you know after I phone her." Brian light-heartedly replied. Louise was fully in favour of Brian helping his mate and reassured him she was still very capable of running the charity without him after having her holiday in the States.

Closing time came and Brian shut and locked the front door, then retreated into the little flat at the back. What Jeff called tucker was not anything like the food Brian was expecting to eat. In containers were a variety of sliced meats, some over-ripe mangoes, a bag of carrots and a tray of chicken kebabs with a dubious use-by date.

"Looks like I ll be eating out tonight, the food in that Italian restaurant was bloody good – reckon I'll give it another go," Brian said to the fridge as he closed its door, "and as luck happens, I can walk to it from here. Just have to put the bike in the shop for the night."

Being a Monday night only a few patrons were dining in Casa Mama. Spare tables were plentiful with the exception of those closest to the self-serve salad bar. Brian opted for a quiet corner where he could observe diners coming and going. After handing a menu to Brian the waiter asked if he would like something to drink. It had been quite some time since alcohol had passed his lips so he opted for a soda squash instead. 'Have to look after the shop tomorrow and the last thing I need would be a hangover headache. Better not have anything stronger,' he mused as he perused the multipage bill-of-fare. 'Pasta, pizza, fish or meat' he asked himself then mumbled. "Italians are renown for the two P's – pasta and pizza, had pasta last time so it is pizza. Mmmm, Pizza Marinara sounds delicious."

Service again was excellent, faster than he expected and his pizza arrived just as he was headed for the salad bar. I reckon a squeeze of lemon would go well on the Marinara he decided.

"Thought you didn't come here very often," a voice from behind said as he tonged two wedges of lemon onto the little plate he was holding. "Hello Brian, dining alone again?" said the voice he had immediately recognised.

"G'day, or should I have said good evening, Cheryl," he replied then stood looking at her for a moment thinking 'Wow!' His inner desire for her completely unnerved Brian as he tried to continue a conversation, then stammered. "J-Jeff's so-called food in his f-fridge would not sustain a fly, so I opted to eat here. A-are you dining with someone?"

The dress Cheryl was wearing highlighted her lovely figure and Brian found it difficult to think of anything else to say.

"No, it is only me by myself tonight," said Cheryl.

"Ha-have you ordered yet?" he nervously spluttered.

"No – just walked in when I saw you across the room," she replied.

Brian stumbled through another uneasy sentence "Have ordered a p-pizza would you like to share with me, Marinara and it lo-looks a bit big just for one person."

"Only if I can pay for half," Cheryl replied, then daintily placed another piece of lemon on his plate.

As they dined Brian related how he had virtually bluffed his day in the bookstore. "I really don't know much about authors and who wrote what. I had a few tricky questions but somehow I was able to give an answer that made the customers happy. I suppose that is what selling is all about – making the customer feel as though they have got a good deal." His train of thought explode into pieces when Cheryl stood up and said:

"Need another piece of lemon" then headed in the direction of the salad bar.

Brian's eyes were riveted on her as he watched her walking away from the table. The dress certainly emphasised her womanly assets. From the very first day he saw her these had not gone un-noticed by him. It had been such a long time since any woman had aroused his interest. Was it love or lust he asked himself and then cheekily answered his own question with the thought "Would I love to jump into bed with her?" Hoping she had not caught him out having a 'perve' he quickly dropped his head down pretending to look at the pizza as she returned to the table. He could feel his heart thumping harder and inhaled a deep breath to settle it back down.

"Are you OK?" Cheryl quizzed him just after he had heavily exhaled.

This brought a flush of red to his cheeks. Then without thinking blurted out, "You look incredibly lovely tonight."

"Thank you, Brian – I was hoping you had noticed," she responded, then lifted another slice of the pizza onto her plate. "Jeff has told me that your wife walked out on you a couple of years ago," she said before taking her next bite of pizza. Then threw the big curve-ball. "Is there any hope of you two getting back together?"

Brian sat deep in thought for a moment or two before replying. "That's a big question. I'm still trying to work that out." He then went on to relate how he had seen her with the other man, the baby and how she turned up with the J.Ws. "I am trying to do what is right, but the answer is not forthcoming for me – her man has died and she is alone – so am I." He said as he slowly shook his head from side to side.

"Have you ever spoken to her about things? Perhaps the answer will be in what she has to say?" Cheryl suggested.

The rest of the meal was eaten quietly. Both deliberated on what thoughts they had about the situation.

"Would you like a lift back to the shop," asked Cheryl as they settled the bill for the pizza.

"I would love to have a ride in the Morris but tonight I need to walk and settle a few things in my head." Brian said as he gave Cheryl a parting peck on the cheek. A hint of an alluring delicate French perfume from Cheryl's neck teased Brian's senses causing him to momentarily pause before he could finish what had intended to say. "T-Thanks for the offer. Can I take a rain-check on that?"

"Raincheck it is then – the thrill of being a passenger in my mighty Morris will just have to wait. Hope the shop customers go easy on you tomorrow," she cheerily replied as she returned a cheek kiss then headed toward the parking area.

As he walked back to the flat his thoughts were not dissimilar to a cage full of monkey's bouncing back and forth from the branches to the wire of the enclosure. Images of Cheryl, Suzanne and the children, Cheryl's dress and his days living on the street flashed around his mind. 'What am I to do?' he asked himself over and over until he reached the shop's front door.

Once inside he made a bee-line for the bed and flopped onto it. Brian's mind was working overtime trying to unlock what the future may hold for him if he pursued Cheryl or made amends with Suzanne. Tuesday morning found him still laying fully clothed on the bed. Thankfully the store did not require opening until 9.30. This gave him enough time to shower and shave and devour a quick breakfast of cereals, toast and tea.

Throughout the day book buyers and browsers came and went. Thankfully Brian received only a couple of tricky questions and somehow managed to provide convincing answers. A few minutes before closing time Jeff phoned to let him know that his father had deteriorated further and was staying with him overnight again. He gave Brian the option to remain and open in the morning or place a notice in the window to inform the customers the shop will be closed until Thursday, when Jillian returns.

"Everything is going good so-far and I reckon I can handle another day of book selling. I'll stay and open up tomorrow, but don't expect me to eat that stuff in the fridge you mistakenly call food," Brian said with a laugh in his voice.

Rather than choose a restaurant to eat at Brian decided to opt for a hamburger at one of the fast food dine-ins. It had been many years since he had sat down to a meal (if one would describe it as) of burger, chips, nuggets and cola. 'Must be going crazy – me eating junk food,' he thought as he munched on a trio of fries. Glancing around the room he could see why many people had a weight problem. Most of the diners were obese parents with overweight kids munging-out on trays loaded with large amounts of the same items. Then he made a mental note. 'Won't be coming back for another ten years – value my health and my wallet more than this stuff.'

Instead of returning to the flat along the same streets Brian opted to meander through a trendy eatery area.

As he walked past a group of people sitting behind the ram-raid protection bollards of a café, one of the diners called out "Hey Ashworth want to join us for a coffee?"

The unexpected invitation caught him completely off-guard. His immediate reaction was to think it was Jeff having a break from his hospital watch, but the voice was not his. Trying to pick out the culprit from the group was made harder as the perpetrator had deliberately hid himself behind another person seated. This made Brian feel like a complete dork – standing on the footpath, looking into a crowd and not recognising anyone or knowing who posed the question. Then one of the group pointed his finger towards where the chap was hidden. This action caused the caller to stand up and be seen. "G'day Sarg – it's me Lance Corporal Jamison." He said as he beckoned for Brian to join the party.

The penny had now dropped as to who Cheryl had spoken with that knew him. After winding his way around the bollards and a past few tables Brian was offered a seat with the group. As he was about to settle on his chair Colin stood up and introduced Brian to the others. "This is my Afghanistan platoon Sergeant, Brian Ashworth. Very brave soldier that always ensured the safety of his men. Haven't seen him since we returned." The he turned towards Brian with an outstretched hand ready for a hand shake.

"It has been a while," Brian replied as he accepted his hand and gave it a hearty shake. Instinctively Brian leaned toward Colin and gave him a man-hug both ending their embrace with the mandatory three slaps on the back. It was Private Colin Jamison back then. "Long time no see, but you had been mentioned in local gossip a few weeks ago," said Brian as he accepted the chair that was being moved towards him.

While sipping on cappuccinos Colin and Brian began chatting about what they had been doing since their service days. Colin was slightly more open and related how he had fallen victim to a heavy bout of post-traumatic-stress after returning from his tour of duty in Afghanistan. While talking Colin confessed the reason he had divorced was because his ex-wife had never understood his personal struggle with war-induced depression.

In a voice loud enough for everyone in the café to hear, Colin unashamedly echoed his feelings, 'Any Politician that thinks sending a soldier to a war zone where they are expected to kill others and in turn, will see their mates being killed, has no idea of the reality of war. To assume a soldier will return home mentally unscathed is pure fantasy by that Government!' Colin could see that his words had a profound effect on his Sergeant and sat silently for almost a minute while Brian cogitated what had just been spoken.

"How did you cope with it all" Brian asked as he looked directly into Colin's eyes. "Mate – thanks to the support of my wonderful family I now have it mostly under control – except for the odd occasion when any sound similar to that of a gunshot – I still shit myself. Thank Christ my folk stood by me or I would have ended up in the loony-bin." Colin declared loud enough again for the others to hear then hit Brian with the question "What about you. Did the dreaded black dog ever sink its teeth into your sanity?"

"As a matter of fact the black mongrel did take a chunk out of me. I tried to hide the fact that I was having problems. My wife couldn't take it, so she split with the kids and everything else." Rather than disclose anything about being on the streets Brian paused as he spooned the last few drops of milk foam from his almost empty cup.

Colin took advantage of the silence and queried Brian. "Suzanne wasn't it? So what are you up to now - found yourself another woman? He asked as he also scooped the remnants of froth from the inside of his mug.

"It's a long story" Brian began to say then altered his course and quizzed Colin with, "How do you know Cheryl?" A big smile grew on Colin's face "I reckon I know now where the local gossip came from," then continued with, "I'm doing mechanics at Dad's garage when this chick in an old Morris Minor arrives at the workshop to have the brakes adjusted. Nearly bashed my head on the bonnet of the Falcon that I was working on when I saw her getting out of her car. Wow! She was gorgeous. When she came back to collect her vehicle I asked her to go on a date with me but she said she was already taken." Then Colin mumbled as his smile subsided, "Lucky bastard that gets her – not only stunning but a real nice chick."

Those words of Cheryl having a partner, instantly changed Brian's desire to stay with Colin's group any longer. Then Brian took a quick look at his watch, "Sorry mate, I must get going – have to work tomorrow" he tendered as an excuse as he rose from his seat. After paying for his coffee and offering to catch up again, left the gathering.

'Already taken', was not the words Brian needed to hear. 'She hasn't said anything about having a man in her life', drifted through his thinking until his mind exploded with an alternate theory. "Christ, she's a Lesbian and Jill is her partner. How dumb am I not to have seen it. They went on that cruise together. Gee I must be bloody blind" he loudly chastising himself as his pace quickened going back to the flat. Getting to sleep that night proved to be a problem as the thought of Cheryl preferring a woman ricocheted around in his head.

In the morning Brian was sitting bleary eyed at the table eating Jeff's half stale rice bubbles. The mere thought of Cheryl being gay was an open wound causing his gut to churn. "She is the only woman that has caught my attention since Suzanne and it looks like I will get nowhere with her. I am trying to do what is right and shit like this hits me straight in the face." He muttered negatively as he tipped what remained of the uneaten sodden cereals into the kitchen sink. "Go with the flow – help others and everything will turn out right, that's bullshit!" He yelled at the ceiling.

Having done a verbal dummy spit brought Brian back to an almost calm attitude. The thought of Cheryl's sexual orientation remained nagging in the back of his mind.

On the dot of ten a.m. Brian opened the bookstore front door and placed the 'now open' sign outside. For a minute he stood watching vehicles passing and the assortment shoppers walking along the footpath when he heard the familiar beep-beep of a car horn. It was the Morris Minor being driven by Jill and was waving at him through the little cars open window a she drove past without stopping. "Another Lesbian?" was his impulsive thought as he waved back.

Throughout the day a steady stream of customers came and went. Being busy helped keep Cheryl and Jill from his thoughts and put a stop to his thinking about the world conspiring against him. That's how it looked to him at this point of time. By closing time he had enough of selling books. 'What I need is a cup of coffee to pick me up or I will be asleep before bedtime,' emerged as his first priority as he locked the front door of the store. After making a stronger than usual mug of instant, Brian sat at the table in the flat, his mind drifted into thinking about the many recent events that had dovetailed into his life 'Is this a test or just crook luck or, are the bastards conspiring to send me back out onto the streets to live again. All I seem to be doing is being tested, so what in hell is happening. It is about time I got some clarity on the direction my life is to go', he was contemplating as the rattle of keys could be heard in the shop door lock.

Jumping up from the table Brian headed towards the shop access door. As his hand touched the doorknob it swung open. The surprise of Jill walking through the doorway caught him off guard.

"Struth, I thought the place was being robbed," Brian managed to splutter.

"Nice way to greet the manager," she replied with a wink then included, "Thought I ought to come and see how things were going and see if there is any banking to be done. I'm on my way to the hospital to check on Father and give Jeff a break."

"There's not much cash – I spent it all, ha! Most people are using plastic and only very few pay with real money. As you can see there is nearly bugger all in the cash box," he cheekily replied whilst still pondering the question of orientation.

"How is the old fellow – will he ever come out of hospital?" Brian asked politely.

"Not sure, it's still fifty-fifty. The results of test they took will be back tomorrow. The doctor will know more when he gets them. What about you – do you reckon you can do another day of flogging books?" Jill enquired as she counted the money from the cash box.

"Louise said she had everything under control back at the

charity. I suppose another day won't kill me," Brian answered, then paused for a moment before he ventured into the area of more importance to him. "Have you seen Cheryl lately – saw you in her car when you waved?"

To which Jill replied, "Like a good sport she left the car at the airport for me. I ll be returning it to her this weekend."

That answer gave no clue as to Jill and Cheryl's relationship.

"Are you two going anywhere on the weekend? the inquisitive Brian asked.

"That depends on what condition Dad is in." She changed the subject. "I've taken out all the large notes to bank and left the small ones for change and if you need some cash for food – got to go as I promised I'd be at the hospital before six. Catch you tomorrow," Jill hurriedly stated on her way out the door.

Not being in the mood for either cooking a meal or dining out that evening, Brian did the lazy thing and ordered a large pizza to be delivered to the flat, thanks to some of the cash Jillian had left. After eating his 'meal' that was big enough for two, Brian lay on the bed feeling a tad bloated. His thoughts drifted, trying to get a grasp on all the things that had happened in quick succession. On his journey through life, he seemed to be facing many challenges each day. More-so now than ever before.

'Where am I headed? Will I ever have another woman in my life?' rattled around in his head. 'All I desire is to love and be loved and stay healthy. It has been a long time since I was truly content. The healthy part is up to me by keeping fit and avoiding rubbish foods,' he mused with a hint of guilt for having devoured the entire pizza.

Next morning a shipment of books had arrived for the shop. Several customers came into the store. It wasn't until the afternoon that Brian had enough time to contact Jeff with a quick phone call to enquire about his father's health, and what to do with the cartons of books. Brian could tell by the tone in Jeff's voice that it was good news regarding his Dad.

"The doctor's seen the results. He's now confident that he can perform a small operation that will extend the old blokes life for at least another few years." Then Jeff laughingly quipped, "Mate, I would be grateful if you could unpack all the boxes and sort the books into author groups for me."

The stack of the books on the counter had partly obscured a section of the shop where a customer was browsing. 'Better attend to the customer' he thought as he flattened another empty carton then stacked it on the growing pile adjacent the rear door.

He walked towards a lady shopper that had her back to him.

"Can I be of some assistance?" Brian offered.

The woman turned around. Both she and Brian stood speechless for several seconds.

"C-C-can I-I help you?" Brian stuttered nervously to the person he now recognised as Suzanne.

The shock of having unexpectedly encountered her ex-husband prevented her from any form of reply. A book she was holding dropped to the floor with a loud thud. This broke her uneasy silence. "Sorry - I'm sorry," was all she could mutter, then pushed past Brian and headed towards the door but stopped before opening it.

Brian's legs had turned to lead. His heart was pounding, his brain was racing trying to think of what to say or do next. Thankfully no other customers were in the store to witness the chance encounter or cause distraction to such a delicate moment.

Suzanne had composed herself much quicker than he could. "Is this your shop?" she politely asked.

Brian could not offer an answer as his thoughts continued to race inside his head. "I – I" was all he could say.

Suzanne's stronger personality took charge of the situation and made an offer for her and Brian to meet after closing time. "I have an appointment to attend but can come back later – there are a few things we should discuss," she said as she opened the door and exited, leaving him with his mouth agape after he managed to mutter, "S-sure – sure".

Seeing Suzanne had the same impact on him as being hit by a freight train. His normal clarity of mind had turned to a blur. His head had become a cement mixer of jumbled thoughts. "Shit!! - Wasn't expecting that - need time to think and regain my composer before she returns," he mumbled as he locked the shop's front entrance and flipped the 'Back in 5 minutes' placard around to face the street and made a bee-line to the flat.

Brian sat at the table with his head cupped in his hands and remained in that position for a minute or two until his anxious breathing had settled. Was this a coincidence or had it been triggered by last night's wondering why things are happening in rapid succession?

"Where did that one come from – it seems if I ask a question, I get an answer – but who would have ever expected one so quick?" he quizzed himself as he slowly regained composure. It was another full hour before closing time. Another nerve wracking hour before Suzanne would return. For Brian it would be sixty minutes of grappling with what to say.

After making himself a mug of coffee he mooched toward the door and flipped around the 'now open' side of the placard and unlocked the door. His desire to keep the store open had totally diminished. The only reason for doing so, was that Suzanne said she would be coming back. Thankfully no customers were waiting to enter. Instead of watching the clock, Brian reluctantly continued to unpack the last few cartons of the delivered books while imagining different scenarios of what attitude he might take on her return. Should I show my affection or disdain for her? Maybe I ought to pretend this is my shop and brag of how successful I have been? Perhaps I should get angry and give her a good telling off, he also mused. None of the ideas fitted the situation due to his newfound empathy for other people.

Only minutes before the store was due to close Suzanne returned and stood near the entrance, probably waiting to see what Brian's intentions were. Possibly in her mind she believed her own lie that he had been rough with her before the estrangement and was reluctant to confront him again.

Upon sighting her, Brian acted surprisingly calm compared with his earlier agitated state. He simply walked past her and removed the A-frame sign from the footpath and brought it into the store. He knew the truth about his perceived composure. He was like a duck on the water. Seemingly calm swimming on the river but underneath the water the feet were paddling franticly against the current. So were his nerves.

"Thanks for coming back," he said as he rested the sign against a nearby shelf. "I've often wondered if we would ever meet again and under what circumstances. I did catch a glimpse of you on a couple of occasions. Once in the park near the river with a man and a baby, then another time months later with some Jehovah Witnesses that came down our street," he said in a quiet yet controlled voice.

"Yes," Suzanne replied, "I saw you looking from the house doorway and I hoped you had not sighted me because I was really a nervous wreck when I went 'Witnessing' with the others. It was the first time I had ever done that."

"Sorry to hear about your bloke and his child – those Witness blokes told me that they had died, when I asked about who you were that day," Brian said sympathetically. "How are the girls?" he enquired, in an effort to quickly shift the subject away from her loss.

For a few seconds Suzanne stood lost in her memories, desperately holding back her grief, then replied to his question in a restrained and matter of fact way.

"They're growing up so quick. Louise is in High School and Mary is in year seven. They ask about you and I don't know what to say. I told them you had gone back to the war. I wish I never had started that lie because they now ask when you are coming home," she said with her head lowered, trying to conceal the up-welling of tears in her eyes as the loss of her baby re-emerged in her thoughts.

Sensing her distress Brian offered her a chair and placed one for himself a few feet away. He sat slouched with his feet extended forward.

Suzanne sat on the edge of her seat then looked down again and said, "I suppose I should say I am sorry," she said meekly.

Brian placed his hands on top of his head, leaned further back, took a deep breath and observed her body language. In front of him he saw a much weaker Suzanne than he had ever seen before. Her demeanour had changed from a demanding and often frighteningly direct woman to one withdrawn and hesitant with a soul laden with guilt. This was not the wife that he often strived to please. For once in his life he felt that the cards were with him. The days of him being a melancholic PTSD sufferer that had allowed himself to become subservient to her dominance vanished the moment he saw that she was also capable of being vulnerable.

An uneasy silence between them held for a minute or two while each contemplated what to say or do next. Having the upper hand Brian put forward the question: "Where to from here?"

Suzanne remained staring at her feet for a few moments longer, then slowly raised her head, looked Brian in the eye and almost floored him with her reply. "Would you become a Jehovah's Witness for me and the girls?"

His mouth dropped open as he contemplated the magnitude of her request.

"What difference would that make?" he somehow managed to ask as a thousand thoughts scrambled across his mind in disbelief of what he had just heard her utter. He had been hoping for nicer questions like, how is your life going? are you well? or, what have you been doing? Or, are you in a relationship?

Her question totally destroyed his previous notion of her being helpless and brought the realisation that apart from mourning her lost child the woman in front of him had not softened her stance. It was still all about her with the mention of the girls thrown in as a guilt lever to retain her dominance.

Suzanne saw the change in Brian's demeanour and instantly realised she had crossed the line of what was should have been a neutral first-encounter. She tried to give herself a plausible reason for her probe. "Since I've been meeting and doing Bible studies with other Witnesses it has been explained to me that having a non-believer in a relationship is acting against the will of Jehovah and that relationship will not be sanctioned by the elders."

Brian leaned forward and cupped his head in his hands in disbelief of what she had just said, then slowly and deliberately posed his own question.

"Do you mean that you, the girls and I cannot be a family again unless I join the JWs? Why should that be a criteria – I'm not interested in what your church tells you – I only care about sorting out where we went wrong and fixing it to become a family again."

The air was thick with emotional tension, both silently searched their minds for how to amicably bow out gracefully from this meeting.

Suzanne broke the lingering quiet with the all too familiar haughty mannerism he remembered. "Brian, you seem so much stronger now – not the weakling you once were. Jehovah has revealed to me that when my partner and child died it was a penance for the sins of failing our marriage then living out of wedlock with another man. I can see that it was part of Jehovah's plan for me."

Then her voice grew colder, almost as if she was repeating words from a book. "Jehovah's word says that the Witnesses will be the only ones saved when the day of Armageddon arrives. I am offering you the chance to be with us in God's Kingdom, to stand beside me and the thousands of Witnesses that will one day inherit Jehovah's new world. Before you say no, come with us to a bible meeting at the Kingdom Hall and you may then understand why I believe that unlike other religions, we have the truth."

'Armageddon' instantly bombarded Brian's headspace. To Brian that single word reflected a belief in a God that was willing to destroy everyone with the exception of those of that one religion. The radical Islamists he had fought against held a similar religious mentality where only they could enter the Kingdom of Heaven. He paused for a long moment. In his mind he pictured the horrific images of suicide bombers in Afghanistan.

Brian took a deep breath then judiciously said, "I have seen what happens when a radical religion uses its followers to turn man against man for not believing in the stuff they teach. Why should I ever believe what your Jehovah's preach and become a doomsday predictor? How often have they stated a date when the world will end? I cannot understand how you have swallowed so much of their religious crap and now believe it."

Suzanne was gob-smacked by his reply and went into defence mode. Her posture changed, her back stiffened as she slid her body to the edge of her chair. She tightened her lips and looked down at Brian and venomously stated – "I gave you a choice. You've made it clear that you don't want what I am offering. I will simply tell the girls that you were killed in action. To me you are already spiritually dead. We don't believe in wars. Because you were a soldier they will come to understand that it was your penalty for killing other humans."

She then rummaged through her handbag and took out a religious tract with the title of 'Jehovah's Family' and shoved it at a stunned Brian. Without waiting for his response, rose to her feet, turned and exited the bookstore.

Being hit by a fast-moving dump truck would have had less impact than Suzanne's outpouring of religious zealousness. Almost ten minutes slipped by before Brian rose from his chair with his head still in constant dialogue with his objective reasoning.

"What the hell has got into her?" he muttered as he re-secured the shop door with the dead-lock. "Brainwashed! They have bloody brainwashed her!" he shouted at the bookshelves.

That night, sleep was never to happen. Today's meeting with Suzanne hurtled his mind into a tangle of thoughts and emotions. It became clear that unless he bowed to her religion based demand there would be no chance of reconciliation. The long held hope of reuniting with Suzanne and having a family once more was inevitably gone? A gut wrenching feeling of being rejected and alone surged through his entire body. His vision blurred as a huge dose of stress driven adrenalin released into his system and threw him into a heart broken sobbing wreck of man that urgently needed someone to hug and hold him and make the anguish of the encounter disappear.

"Hey, Wake up mate – it is past opening time. Were you been on the piss last night? You look bloody terrible," Jeff said as he shook Brian's shoulder.

It was indeed half an hour beyond the shop's appointed opening time. A customer had phoned Jill to inquire if the shop was going to be closed all day. Jill rang Jeff and asked him to check on Brian on the way to the hospital. The total preoccupation with yesterday's episode, Brian had failed to set the alarm. He had fallen into a deep sleep around dawn.

Brian sat on the edge of the bed and gave Jeff a brief run-down of the previous day.

"She must have totally flipped to get sucked in like that – why has she started believing all that religious claptrap?" Jeff said as he tried to console Brian, then went on to say, "I'll give Jill a call and she can look after the shop today. I'll wait until she gets here and then go and see Dad. And you mate, you need to get some fresh air and get out of the place for the rest of the day. Why don't you give the bike a run, maybe ride down to the bay and fill your lungs with a hearty gulp of salty air. It's great for clearing the mind and you certainly need to do just that."

The roar of the motor and a firm grip of the throttle, the foot flicking the gear lever through its notches worked better than a dose of anti-depressant to release the angst of the Suzanne experience. After a mood revitalising ride down the highway Brian arrived at seaside. Parked the BMW in a four hour zone and secured his helmet in the frame lock. His mind had already begun to settle, his sunglasses hid his tired and reddened eyes.

A frothy cappuccino would go down well, he mused, as he neared a row of cafés and coffee shops. Choosing a table with an un-interrupted view of the adjacent park he sat taking in the sights and sounds of the area. Children frolicked in the water squirting fountain while parents casually watched from the benches nearby. His thoughts were lost in seeing the happiness of the kids playing, knowing full well that the protection of a mum or dad were close at hand. Suzanne's words began to creep back into his mind. "If you want us to be a family again then you must become a Jehovah Witness." Before he could add another suggestion to his brain-space, he was timely interrupted by, "Would you like to order now sir?" With a quick shake of his head to bring himself back to earth Brian ordered a double shot cappuccino in a mug with plenty of froth.

Brian lingered over his coffee taking his time relishing every sip then spooning the remnants of the creamy foam slowly into his mouth while gazing at the scene of people relaxing and being happy. This was his turning point. He had long held an inner belief that one day his family and he would be reunited. The encounter with Suzanne and her stipulation for him to be subject to her demands finally bought that to an end. The woman is totally off the list of a wanted partner – no way could I ever become one of those fruit-loops to which she has aligned herself. She had previously isolated the girls, ripped him off and destroyed his life. Her stipulation to follow her religion put the lid on ever being reunited. It was time to start a new life.

The weight finally lifted from his shoulders of his perceived love for her. A realisation that she held no true love for him was manifestly obvious. No longer was he a pawn in her selfish game. Now his spirit was free and a new journey was about to start.

Brian resolved to seek an uncomplicated life. Take time off for relaxing. Arrange weekends to mingle among others doing the same. Live without stress. Have a partner by his side who held no desire to control his life. From this point onwards his aim would be to find a woman that he could share his love and she would love him in return.

The possibility of Suzanne returning to the bookstore with more ultimatums unnerved Brian. Jeff readily agreed that he should no longer need to help with the shop. He recognised that his mate was going through difficult times and accepted the fact that Jill and he would once again have to take turns in operating the business and doing the hospital visits without Brian's help. Louise was delighted when Brian phoned her and said his stint at the bookshop was over.

A new episode was about to begin for Brian toward finding contentment. Back working with Louise and the other team members at the charity kitchen placed a fresh perspective on caring for the unfortunates of society. Through his own adversity the true value of giving love unconditionally had been instilled into his life.

Now added to Brian's day was the giving of words of encouragement to those homeless ones having weightier than usual difficulties. More often his problem solving and timely advice was heeded than overlooked. The passion for inspiring the poor to strive to reenter society had not gone un-noticed.

Louise was seriously considering retiring from being manager of the kitchen and she had put forward Brian's name as a suitable replacement. The institution heads acknowledged Lou's choice and offered Brian the job that would also entail overseeing a counselling programme the Government were funding through the charity. This time the position came with a salary instead of being an unpaid volunteer as he had done for almost two years.

Brian was humbled by the recognition and at the same time delighted to be receiving an income.

"Perhaps I'll be able to pay you some rent now that I'm able to afford it," Brian said to Lou one morning. "Maybe even look around and find a house to lease if you would like me out," he added.

Louise smiled and said, "I know where there is a very nice place you may like – it's close to your work and the rent is modest."

Brian responded, "I'll be sad to leave your place. It's the only place that has the spirit of Roy keeping watch over the property. Whenever I have been feeling low – sitting for a moment in the cabin always returns calmness to my soul. He must have been a saint of man."

"Quite so," said Lou in return. "You and Roy are so similar – you both have a wonderful empathy for others and at the same time need also to be appreciated. I do hope that one day someone will bring you the love you deserve. I did truly love Roy with all my heart and…" then tapered off as a tear began to roll down her cheek.

With the assistance of a Brian's caring arm around her shoulder, it took Lou about a minute to regain her composure.

"Maybe we should talk about paying rent and houses some other time," he suggested.

Lou directly looked him in the eyes. "I would rather we talked now," she replied. Then, in a matter of fact way, said "Now that I will have spare time, I'm thinking of flying back to the United States to stay with my cousin for a year, or even longer. Perhaps spend some of it teaching her how to cook the Australian way. Heavens knows why they eat so much junk over there. Apart from all the food, I would like to see more of America. Take a bus tour to the East Coast with her and have a look at the Big Apple New York, and see the Statue of Liberty." Then she lingered for a moment, "Brian how would you like to have my house for the year. The rent will be minimal - just enough to cover the cost of the gardener coming in to do the lawns and pay the Council rates. One condition, all my personal stuff such as clothes, my ornaments and my beautiful pictures of Roy will have to be locked away in my bedroom, the rest of the place is yours to use. How about it?"

It had been quite some time since the more pleasant elements of living rolled Brian's way. Being more content had kept the dreaded Black Dog at bay. A paid position at the Charity and now an offer to rent Lou's house was an added bonus. Without hesitation Brian jumped at the opportunity.

"Lou, you have a heart of pure gold – yes, would love to stay. I promise to look after your home. I have always felt at home here." Then to express his gratitude gave her a big hug.

After Lou departed for America, Brian developed a week-day routine of going to work and coming home, eating supper, watching television, then retreating to bed. Weekends were spent washing clothes then planning strategies for adopting programmes for the following week, of ways to assist the homeless. Two months flittered past without a break from the humdrum of this routine.

Brian had become fully immersed in his work with the aim of proving to himself that he was once again a worthy employee. Supplementary care programmes were running smoothly and the kitchen continued feeding the homeless which now was staffed with a full complement of volunteers thanks to his recruitment initiatives. This was not the intended direction he hoped to be heading. Where was the interaction with other people on weekends? Brian made the decision that the next weekend he would grasp the opportunity and make time to relax.

Breakfast at the seaside was chosen as Saturday morning's priority. A small problem arose when he discovered the motorbike battery had gone flat through lack of use. A recharge was needed. Thankfully Roy's old 12 volt charger was still in the garage. It would take some time to input enough power to start the BMW's engine.

Having the forced delay, Brian decided that a bowl of cereal would go down well as a temporary hunger stopper to hold him over to what now would be brunch. With the cornflakes in the bowl, he was about to pour on the milk when a 'Beep-beep' echoed from the driveway. A glance out of the window revealed it was Cheryl climbing out of her little Morris Minor. The flash of thought of how attractive she looked in her jeans and jumper was over-ridden by his thinking that she preferred other woman.

"Long time no see," Cheryl quipped as he met her at the front door. "Been a while – lots of changes since I last set eyes on you," Brian said as he beckoned her to enter the house. "Have you had breakfast yet?" he asked as he lifted the cereal packet above a clean empty bowl.

"No thanks – had mine already," Cheryl said as she sat at the table.

"What do I owe the pleasure for today's visit?" he asked spooning some cereal into his mouth, then continued to talk with a mouth full, "Everything alright? Is Jeff's dad still kicking?"

"Yes, everyone is doing fine. Pop's over his health problems and now trying to give Jeff advice from his wheel chair on how to run the bookstore. He is back to his old self," smiled Cheryl then continued with, "None of us had seen or heard from you for weeks. Thought I had better come and check that you had gotten over the ex-wife saga Jill told me about."

Brian was taken aback by what Cheryl had just said and wondered what Jill had imparted to her. He paused eating his breakfast and sheepishly offered his excuse of being so occupied with his new job he had failed to remember his friends.

"What new job is that?" Cheryl enquired.

"Seems I had slipped up on that as well – I have been appointed the manager of a care program at the Charity. Been slaving away to put a new agenda into practice. All that and more, plus looking after the house has kept me busy."

"Where is Louise – nothing wrong with her, is there?" quizzed Cheryl.

"Lou's in the USA and I am renting the house for a year, so I'm trying to keep it as neat as she would like it to be," he said as he mouthed the last few spoonsful of cereal. "Was going down to the bay for a café breakfast but the motorbike battery was dead and now it's recharging. Would you like a coffee," Brian offered Cheryl.

"Here or at the bay?" she replied.

"I meant here – but if you like to wait for about five minutes – we can ride to seaside – providing I can start the Beamer. The bike desperately needs a run, it appears I had not only forgotten my mates but the bike as well," Brian said as washed the breakfast bowl.

"Haven't been on a motorbike for years – not sure if I will be scared," Cheryl replied in a girlish voice.

Unsure whether Cheryl was actually scared or not, Brian felt a surge of pleasure that increased his pulse rate, when she wrapped her arms firmly around him as they started to motor down the highway, then remained that way for the entire journey. Many years had passed since he was hugged by an attractive woman. This single act of affection or whatever her intentions stirred the maleness in him, an interaction that had been missing from his life.

"How was that – were you scared or just hanging on tightly?" Brian asked her as they dismounted at their destination.

A flush of red glossed over Cheryl's cheeks as she removed her helmet and answered, "Just a little bit at first," then deliberately pointed to a café across the plaza to avoid any further talk. "That's where they make the most scrumptious seafood pizzas, have you ever tried one?"

"I will have to take your word for it – shall we share one for lunch?" Brian asked as he clipped both helmets in the security lock.

"Love to," was all she said as they began walking.

"Shall we wander along the promenade before we eat?" Brian suggested.

To which Cheryl replied, "Good idea," then grabbed Brian's arm as they crossed the street and headed towards the beach front.

The mixed signals Brian was receiving from Cheryl created some doubt as to intentions. Was she being just friendly or was she showing some sort of affection for him?

"Afraid you will get run over?" he asked as they reached the opposite footpath.

This question startled Cheryl and she immediately let his arm free. Then politely said "Seemed to be the right thing for me to do – a girl needs protection." Then giggled and gave him a small punch on the arm. The remainder of the walk Cheryl kept a respectable but still close distance from him, except when it necessitated her to take hold of his arm again in order to avoid some family groups also taking a stroll.

At the café the pizza and coffees were ordered. Cheryl sat directly opposite Brian and fiddle with a fork, twisting it round and round, often glancing among the passers-by. Brian followed her eye direction trying to figure out what she was looking at. He noticed her glimpses were held longer on the young woman that walked past. Another mental flash of females being her preference, crossed his thoughts.

The pizza topped with prawns, calamari, mussels and oysters was as yummy as Cheryl had predicted and was totally devoured before their coffee had a chance to get cold.

"That was delicious, good choice," Brian said as he sipped his latte.

"Perhaps we can do it again with Jill and Jeff next time. I know Jill will want to – we have been here together a few times and she just loves those pizzas," Cheryl suggested.

Brian's thoughts immediately pictured Jill and Cheryl doing a little more than just socializing, then put forward "Maybe I might bring someone too – I could ask the two nice lookers in the shop near where I work. One for me and one for Jeff."

What started out as a pleasant morning suddenly curdled after Brian's last statement.

"Am I not good enough for you?" Cheryl said raising her voice.

"But, but" stammered Brian and before he could finish the remainder of his sentence, Cheryl, now obviously angry, rose from the table then began to walk away,

"You can go back alone, I will catch a tram."

Brian was dumbfounded. "W-W-wait," he stammered as tried to stand and clumsily knocked over the remainder of his drink.

Cheryl was not listening as she hastily made a bee-line for toward the tram stop.

"What's got into her – all I said was that I might bring someone else – what was wrong with that??" Brian said to himself. "She's got Jill, so what is the big deal?" he thought as he tried to mop up the spilled coffee that now covered most of the table.

An explanation from Cheryl was warranted he thought. Brian's immediate reaction was to head for home to meet her in the driveway when she came to collect the Morris. Rather than what might turn out to be a confrontation with her he opted to take a ride along the seafront esplanade and enjoy the remainder of the morning and leave her stew in her moodiness.

It was almost perfect weather, having no rush to go home he chose to dawdle along with his helmet visor up. He could smell the pleasant aroma that drifted from the sea. It reminded him of his life prior to getting married. The freedom riding a motorbike, the smell of the ocean and the warm sun was in total contrast to being with a moody female. 'Perhaps I should forget about having a partner and simply live my life for myself, doing what I want, whenever I want, I had no woman problems when I was single', he mused as he rode further south.

The old Morris was gone from the driveway when he arrived home later that afternoon. A note was rolled up and jammed in the iron work of the front screen door. It simply read, "Sorry – hope to catch up with you again."

Numbers of homeless persons in the region was on the increase. The new support programme was operating better than expected. Word had passed among the unfortunates that a monetary handout could be gotten from the charity. This false information dramatically raised the number of applicants Brian had to deal with. Once again a repetitive home and work schedule took precedence to having leisure time and enjoying weekends with friends.

Jeff was the first one to re-establish contact with an invitation for Brian to help celebrate his Father's eightieth birthday the following Saturday.

"It would be an opportune time for you to meet him – he won't be falling in and out of consciousness. The old bugger is doing well and looking forward to having a party," Jeff joked. "I have booked the restaurant for a 7.30 roll call, probably be only close friends. Will you be coming?"

"Yeh mate, it would be great to catch up with you again."

Brian replied.

Then Jeff responded, "Righto Sarg, see ya Saturday," and hung up before Brian could ask 'where?'

In the past Jeff did not own a phone. 'No need to have one,' he often joked. More often than not, Jeff managed to con a free call from anyone that had a phone handy, therefore Brian had no number to reach him. It took a few minutes for Brian to realise, with a press of the recall button he could reconnect with the phone from which Jeff had called. The phone rang for a few seconds before it was answered.

"Hello – Jill speaking".

"Hi Jill – Brian here."

"Hi Brian".

"Hey Jill – Jeff rang about a party for your dad but never said what restaurant it would be."

"That's just like him – full of detail but low on facts, it will be at our regular eating place, Casa Mama – do you know where that is?"

"Sure do – I have dined there before," then while his thoughts whipped back to the restaurant and Cheryl wearing that form fitting dress, Jill said:

"Sorry Brian, got a customer, can't stop to chat, I have to go – catch up with you Saturday – bye," then hung up.

Needing a well-earned break from the repetitiveness of his employment Brian was looking forward to Saturday's meeting with friends at Casa Mama. Walking to the venue met his strict rule of never to ride a motorbike when drinking alcohol. When he was about eighty metres from the restaurant he watched a man and a woman alight from a taxi, then enter the place holding hands. 'That looked like Jill – but who was the bloke?'

he pondered. Brian confirmed it was Jill when he saw her talking to the maître d near the dining room entrance. The mystery man remained unsighted.

"Hi Brian, glad you could make it," Jill greeted him as he approached her.

"Is Jeff here yet?" Brian asked as he gave Jilly a friendly 'happy to see you too' kiss on her cheek.

"No not yet – he is fetching Dad, but will be here soon." As Brian turned away from Jill, her anonymous escort came through the doorway carrying two glasses of white wine. In an instant Brian recognised him to be none other than Corporal Colin Jamison. With a puzzled look, Brian turned to Jill who immediately introduced her companion. "Brian, this is my boyfriend Colin."

Not one but two initial surprises nearly floored Brian. First one, it became apparent that Jill may not be a lesbian as he had assumed. The other was the bloke she had chosen. Colin in his usual boisterous mannerism, gave Brian a slap on the back, then saluted him and without pausing for a breath, related how he and 'his Sergeant' had served in Afghanistan. The fact they knew each other astonished Jill who then enlightened Brian. They met when she had done a favour and delivered Cheryl's car to the garage for her. Since then they had been dating and had plans to become engaged in month or two. "Have to wait for the ring to get restyled – it was my mother's, a bit old fashioned, so Colin is paying for it to be updated"

The trio ambled towards a table that Jeff had reserved for the night. Brian noted the number of chairs then asked "Booked for six eh! Is Cheryl coming?"

Jill gave a reply, "Cheryl is going to a friend's party first and is hoping to get here a bit later on. I don't know what is rattling her can, did something happen between you and her the other week? She has been acting oddly and will not say why."

Brian provided a run-down of his time with Cheryl.

"Don't really know what I said? We were chatting about getting us all together and having a group breakfast at the bay. She mumbled something about not being good enough then jumped up and stormed off and took a tram back to the city. Haven't seen or heard from her since then. Buggered if I know what she was on about," Brian explained.

"Perhaps you might patch things up tonight" recommended Jill.

Within minutes, Jeff arrived pushing his dad in a wheel chair and settled him at the table. Brian deliberately chose to sit between Jill and her brother Jeff opposite the vacant seat. Subconsciously he was hiding from Cheryl, yet every minute or two, looked toward the door anticipating her entry. The meal eaten and plates cleared it was now time for the birthday cake to be bought to the table. Knowing this, Jill stated she would text Cheryl and tell her to 'get her arse over here – it is cut the cake time'.

Within an instant Cheryl's reply was received. 'Won't be able to make it – still eating at this party – give ya dad a kiss from me'.

"Looks as if we won't be seeing Cheryl tonight," Jill announced as she leaned over to her father and kissed his cheek, "Dad, that's from Cheryl."

After the candle blowing and eating of the cake was over, Jeff offered Colin, Jill and Brian a lift home. "Got a loan of a minibus in case we needed one - so there will be plenty of vacant seats."

"Thanks, but no thanks, we are going to play on a bit longer – there is band playing in the pub up the street. Jill and I will walk there mate. Want to tag along with us Sarg, you never know – you might get lucky there," offered a playful and looking for more fun, Colin.

"Might as well, it will be just me and telly at home," replied a deflated Brian that needed more than his own company.

A packed room full of ravers with loud head-banger music was not what Brian was expecting. Left standing alone at the bar with a half flat beer in his hand like a Nigel Nobody, did nothing to make his night out any happier. When there was a momentary pause in the doof-doof thump of the cacophony, Brian decided enough was enough and found Colin and Jill to tell them he was going home. The 'music' started again which required him to yell in Colin's ear in order to be heard.

"Not my scene - going home – catch up with you soon."

Colin mouthed some only partly audible words in return, "Ok see ya later," then something about Cheryl he could not decipher. Brian tried making sense of what Col had yelled and tried several times to ask him to repeat it, but gave up when another couple pushed between them and started gyrating to the ear deafening beat.

Outside the pub the sound of the band could still be heard although somewhat more muted. Fifty metres down the path a faint bass thump continued to carry in the still night air. Unexpectedly a 'Beep – beep' came from a new looking silver SUV doing a U-turn from the opposite lane then pulled alongside where Brian was standing and looking around trying to determine for whom the beeps were meant.

The passenger window electric motor whirred as the glass slide downward. "Hello stranger," came the familiar voice of Cheryl from the driver's side of the vehicle. "Want a lift?"

"Got yourself a new car?" Brian asked a he opened the

passenger-side door then sat inside.

"Not so lucky – belongs to my mother, having a loan of it while she is in Darwin," Cheryl said, then added "Where are you going? – hope you're not being a party-pooper and heading home? Jill left her phone on the restaurant table, when I called to see if you were still there, Jeff answered and told me three of you had gone to the pub. He had picked up her phone and was going to return it tomorrow. Lucky I saw you walking – otherwise would have missed you. I was coming to join you."

"I was going home. Couldn't take that loud music or 'whatever they call it' back at the pub. Would have been made deaf if I stayed much longer."

"It's not my scene either," agreed Cheryl, then posed an unexpected question. "Would you like to have a drink somewhere? I know a quiet bar not far from here. They make the nicest cocktails, or…" Cheryl then paused for brief moment, "would you rather we have a coffee at your place, so I can apologise for my stuffing up your weekend?"

Brian nervously responded. "I - I reckon home sounds the better option – only got Instant, but do have some flavoured teas that Louise left in the cupboard."

Lemon Myrtle tea, sweetened with honey was chosen as the drink of choice, brewed and poured into mugs then placed on the kitchen table.

Cheryl seated herself on the chair closest to Brian, then sipped at her hot drink, looked up at him then started giving her apologies. "I am sorry I was so uptight on the weekend. In my mind I was hoping that you wanted to be with me but when you said you were going to look for someone else, I cracked." She hesitated for a brief moment before continuing, "Sometime ago I was parked across the road from the Bookshop. In my rear vision mirror I watched you sitting on your motorbike. I wondered if you were waiting for someone. My curiosity as to who you were and that you were waiting for Jill's brother was answered when Jeff brought you into the shop. I nearly wet myself when we were introduced. Do you believe in love at first sight?"

"Love at first sight scares me a bit. Fell in love with my ex Suzanne, the very first time I laid eyes on her. Never expected her to put me through hell. Not sure what to believe anymore," Brian said in a pained voice, then extended his answer. "My first impression of you when you got out of the old Morris was 'Wow, I like what I see' and I still think the same way. I never tried my luck to become more than friends. Thought you and Jill were, how I should say, 'partners'. Still had thoughts that way until tonight, right up to when I saw Colin with Jill. That was my reason for saying I might look for someone, the morning you chucked a wobbly."

Cheryl's face had a distinct pink flush when she replied in a slightly angry tone. "What made you think we were in a relationship? Lesbians, is that what you mean?"

To which Brian answered, "Never saw either of you with a bloke, it was always just the two of you together. The cruise you both went on, didn't help my thinking."

"Let's see. All the time you reckoned I was gay and at the same time, I thought you were in love with your ex-wife. Come to think of it, never saw you with any other woman, only Jeff. Perhaps I should have marked you down as being a pair of poofs. Looks like we were equally wrong having inaccurate opinions of each other," suggested Cheryl.

"Seems I have stuffed up by wrongly judging women," said

Brian as he rolled his mug back and forth between his hands. "I saw things in Afghanistan that played havoc with my brain big time. Wasn't in a good place mentally in those days. When I came back, I tried to hide the emotional stress I was under. My attempts to keep the family together failed. The day Suzanne walked out on me, my world fell apart. Ever since, it has been one heck of a journey. In my heart I wanted to reconcile with my family. It is now obvious that is never going to be. The ex is a control freak and still wants to manipulate. She's gone bonkers with a religion that filled her head with garbage. Deep inside me, I would be afraid of having another attempt of living with her – or anyone else. Big brave Sergeant Brian Ashworth is pooping himself, scared stiff that he will get hurt again."

Cheryl reached out and held the hand that Brian had released from holding the mug and said "I have been in love with you from the moment I first met you. That day we were introduced in the book store something inside me said, this is the man for you, he will give you all the love you need." She paused and gently squeezed his hand then said, "So where to from here – got any ideas?"

Brian stared at the ceiling for a second or two then looked directly at her and said: "For a long time my life has never seen real love. I need loving and need to have someone I can love. You have always been in my mind as that person but I put obstacles in the way. The other day when we were on the bike and you had your arms around me, I wished that you were really hugging me, not just hanging on because you were scared. I wanted so much to hug you back but the thought of you preferring to bat for the other team stopped me."

Cheryl stood up from her chair and coerced Brian to do the same. "You can hug me now," she said softly as her arms slipped behind him. Automatically his arms wrapped around her.

A minute passed before either spoke. Their closeness conveyed more than words. Her warmth and softness, the hint of the same enticing perfume she previously wore that time at the restaurant heightened the pleasure of her nearness. These all combined to cause Brian's heart to involuntarily begin beating much louder than usual.

Cheryl broke the previous intimate silence. "I can feel and hear your heart pounding through your shirt."

"When we were on the motorbike and you put your arms around me, you would have felt my heart thumping just as hard that day too. You have always had that impact on me," Brian said as his head turned, paused for a moment against Cheryl's cheek before giving her a soft lingering kiss. They tightly held each other again, mesmerised in the sensuality of the moment.

"Phew! – Looks like you have the same effect on me, my heart is going bananas as well," Cheryl said as their arms slowly released and she placed her hand over her heart.

"I've been an idiot," Brian admitted as he snuggled his head against hers. "All the time I was trying to do what I believed to be right. I lived in the vain hope of reconciling with the family. Yet I could not see that you were always there waiting so patiently – I feel like a blind bloody idiot."

At that point she took hold of his hands and stood a little apart, looked him in the eyes and said, "You were never a fool, I can understand why you felt that way. Years ago I too thought I was in love. The man who I naively believed to be in love with me, was having an affair behind my back and dumped me for her. I was hurt badly, that is why you only saw me with Jill or a few other female friends. Jilly has been my long-time best friend and always will be. Over the years both you and I have had a rough trot. Let's forget the past, look to our future so we can be happy together." She snuggled into his arms for another extended kiss.

Their passionate embraces were stalled when Cheryl brought them back to reality when she looked at her watch.

"Unfortunately I must go. Have to collect mother from the airport in just over an hour. She is coming home on the 'red-eye' flight from up north. I truly would have loved to stay the night with you. We will just have to until next week for dessert."

Brian looked into her eyes and quietly said, "I have waited for so long for this day – reckon I can survive for another week. You have already made my dreams come true," then he kissed her forehead as he reached for her hand.

Holding hands with their fingers interlocked, only releasing their clasp when they were standing alongside Cheryl's mother's car parked in the driveway.

"I will never ever forget tonight, you have made my dreams become a reality," Cheryl said tenderly as they held each other close then melted into another lingering kiss.

"I love you," Cheryl said as she entered the car then clipped her seat belt on.

"Love you too," Brian replied, then sneaked another kiss through the open window as Cheryl started the engine.

Brian paused in the gateway waving and watching Cheryl drive away. The smile on his face broadened even more as the realisation he would no longer be devoid of a loving partner. Then his mind drifted back to the ending of a poem he had read some time ago when he first sat in the garden hut.

"Someone who is more than a lover, more than just a friend, someone who will be with you, until the very end."

With those poetic words coupled with Cheryl's 'I Love You'

the years that had been a mosaic of depression, hardship, homelessness, plus many personal challenges were finally ending. The arduous lesson of life that he underwent, had bought him to a point of time when the gift of happiness was his to accept. This part of his earthly odyssey had finally arrived where the deep emotional pain of separation was to be replaced this time, with a genuine love and a caring soulmate.

For a long minute Brian stood contemplating the magnitude of the moment before walking back to the house. As he turned around, a feeling of being watched caused him to glance across the street. It was then he sighted a man with an old black dog at his side, both peering in his direction from under a dim streetlight on the opposite footpath. For a fleeting moment Brian thought the mysterious onlooker appeared to be someone familiar. Perhaps it was simply that he closely resembled the Roy he had seen in many of Louise's old photographs.

Being near to midnight also prompted him to wonder why a person would be out walking a dog at such a late hour. While pondering 'why', the man smiled, raised his hand slightly then made a gesture of recognition toward Brian, then both the man and dog silently dissolved like a mist into the ink of the night.

Bewildered by the pair's sudden disappearance Brian's eyes were drawn toward where they were standing. Something on the ground glinted in the moonlight. Out of curiosity he crossed over the road to investigate the shiny object. On the verge among the grass lay an old fountain pen. Brian picked it up then carried it back to the house to have a closer inspection under better lighting.

Once inside the house he could see the embossed pattern on the gold casing was somewhat worn through years of use. Then he rolled it over he could make out what appeared to be someone's initials stylishly engraved into the barrel.

With a little spittle on the area and a quick wipe with his thumb, three letters were revealed – *G R W*.

The Journey

Along the path of life we wander
Looking here and there,
Searching for that someone,
Someone who will really care.

Someone who will love you,
No matter what you do,
Someone who will be there
To help you see life through.

Someone with a quiet strength
With a heart of pure gold,
Someone who can see your needs,
Never having to be told.

Someone who does understand
Errors are a part of learning,
Someone to gently guide your steps
To help stop those faults returning.

Someone who shall only see,
Good in what you have done.
Someone who really knows
How the race of life is won.

Someone who is more than a lover
More than just a friend,
Someone who will be with you
… until the very end.

dennis lightfoot © 1992